THE Last Witch

An

Earth Magic Grimoire

Volume 1

T Wells Brown

The Last Witch: An Earth Magic Grimoire by T Wells
Brown
Published by Terry Wells-Brown
PO Box 132 Woodbridge, Ca. 95258
www.twellsbrown.com
Copyright © 2021 T Wells Brown
For information contact :
 Women of Wine Country
PO Box 132
Woodbridge Ca 95258

Cover by: Terry Wells-Brown
Editor: Heather Osborne
Beta Readers: Don Brown, Brandon Brown, Cyle Kris,
Cynthia Vazquez, Verna Wisner
Proof Readers: Donna Walker, Janette Shutts

ISBN: 978-1-7333309-9-4(2021)

Printed in: United States of America

10 9 8 7 6 5 4 3 2 1

Cool Stuff

Come join me on social media,

Facebook: T Wells Brown

Instagram: @Twellsbrown

Twitter: @twellsbrown

Book Bub: Author T Wells Brown

Stay in the know by signing up for my Newsletter:

www.womenofwinecountry.com

Please follow my author page on

Amazon @ T Wells Brown

Stay tuned for the next volume of the Earth Magic

saga: Sharp Stones coming Spring 2022

Dedication

This modern fantasy tale is dedicated to Wendy and Craig Martelle. The

wonderful souls who adopted my sweet pup, Stanley. They are giving him

the best life; any good boy could ever hope for. If you're curious about his

story, you can find Stanley the Alaskan Dog on Facebook... yes, he has his

own fan club.

Wendy teaches Russian and Spanish in Alaska, and Craig Martelle has

nearly one hundred published books.

Go check him out!

Acknowledgements

To say it takes a small village to produce my books would not be an understatement. From my family; who listen to my story ideas, to my amazing hubby; who reads the very first roughest draft imaginable, to the beta readers, editors, and proofreaders; these books couldn't happen without you. A piece of you is in each one. I will always be grateful for you, and your contribution. I know how blessed I am to have such an incredible literary army at my back.

Heather Osborne for editing for me under the gun, thank you. You made it fun!

Beta Readers; Cyle Kris, Cynthia Vazquez, and Verna Wisner, I couldn't do this without you. Thank you so much!

Proofreaders extraordinaire; my two secret weapons, Donna Walker and Janette Shutts, I love you ladies. I'd be lost without you.

My son Brandon for all of his vast knowledge and understanding of the fantasy world and challenging me to step up. I thank you for helping me become better.

And last, but never least, the Man of my Dreams; there aren't enough words to convey how much your support means. You hold me up.

Serafina the Silent

Elsie the Last Witch

Chapter 1

Place bane jars around the perimeter of your home to keep evil doers and those who'd wish you harm away.

T hick pitted glass blew inward with an angry force. Jars

and bottles flew from the shelf lined walls and crashed to the floor. Wards triggered alarms in the ancient manor and alerted the occupant of intruders, who attacked swiftly in the middle of the night.

An old woman raced up a wooden staircase that led to the highest point of the home.

She stopped at the attic door, placing her open palm against the heavily carved redwood, then hissed and snatched her hand away. She took a step back, narrowing her eyes at the door. Thieves of the peace and tranquility that had been a comforting constant for centuries, were now here.

"So it begins," she whispered.

Bracing herself, she stepped through the doorway.

She was dismayed to see her favorite drying chamber was a complete disaster. Several small black twisters whipped around the room, dislodging anything they came in contact with. Her herbs and spices were ruined. Her two hundred and fifty-seven-year-old herb journal was in the process of being ripped to shreds. All the contents of the room were lost. Even if by chance one or two of the bottles made it out unbroken, she'd never risk that the dirty magic hadn't tainted their contents.

The seemingly frail, elderly woman moved through the broken glass carefully to the center of the room and covered her ears.

"*Senti lesta beline soricori,*" she chanted in a low voice.

Dark tentacles of acrid smoke and foul magic swirled violently. Lightning struck outside the now glassless window, and rain began to pour in. The air was so cold, it made her bones ache as it whipped through her hair and clothes.

She quickly wove her gnarled hands in an intricate pattern directly in front of her face.

White puffs of frigid air escaped her mouth as she continued to chant, "*Senti lesta beline soricori,*" in a low deep voice.

A tree branch crashed into the open window, crushing part of the wall and roofline. The gusting wind increased in ferocity, and ice crystals formed on the pitched ceiling.

Her hands widened and pulled back to her chest as she continued weaving patterns and chanting.

Her voice grew louder, *"Senti lesta beline soricori."* The wind increased its pressure against her body in an effort to drown her out.

She revolved her palms and thrust them away from her chest as her voice continued to grow.

An angry screech sounded above her.

A dark mass formed at the highest point of the ceiling. An entire season's worth of herbs had been hanging from the high wooden beams. That was going to set her back. She completed a full circle, shouting her chant above the roar of the strengthening wind. Her arms spread wide.

They'd forgotten who their opponent was. Who she was. If they'd remembered the lessons of the past, they would not be here, this eve, in this attic, waging war against her.

She continued moving her hands, increasing speed. Sparks of all imaginable shades of blue and green flew from her fingertips. She brought her palms together with a loud clap and yelled, "Ye shall know your foe!"

Her long iron-hued hair rose to dance with the current she was now controlling around her. The magic she commanded grew in its intensity, casting a bright blue glow over the walls of the small room. Her eyes transformed to a luminescent silver and lost their cloudy cover of age. Their focus was bright, sure, and strong.

Who would come for an old woman in the middle of the night? What treachery would bring an end to the quiet bliss the last few centuries had gifted the old witch? It seemed her respite from the war's long past was at an end.

She felt the dark strands of the foul magic attempting to work its way into her mind, spirit, and soul. She'd not encountered this type of magic for centuries.

Tilting her head and raising her chest, she searched for the identity of her attacker.

It seemed familiar. She thought she recognized the signature of the power working so hard to diffuse her ancient magic. An old foe reborn? Or had they survived all these centuries unnoticed, just as she had?

Straightening her bent frame, she called to the ancestors who had come before her. She summoned the spirits of the witches who had once fought the ancient battles that had constantly threatened the world and humankind. She called to the women who had battled and sacrificed.

Vertebrae by vertebrae, she lengthened her aged body gradually, so as not to be noticed by her attackers. It was important, in any conflict, to downplay your strengths and take your opponent by surprise. It was a smart tactical approach that she'd used in hundreds of battles so very long ago. She wondered if this foe had studied her and her strategies. Or would they be emboldened by the physical shell she currently wore?

Fools.

The small twisters raced around the ceiling, merging together and then breaking off to race around again. Bits of wood from the rafters, twigs, leaves and small shards of glass whipped around the room. The witch remained untouched, other than the ice crystals that were forming unnoticed under her bare feet.

Three of the twisters collided at once, and a small explosion of toxic green fire erupted before a wraith appeared from the flame. The creature was completely devoid of light, the blackest black she'd ever seen. It had no eyes or face that she could see, just a flowing form of everything that represented death. The smell of decaying meat filled the small attic. She could feel the power of the ghastly creature as it headed toward her. She threw up a protection ward, hurling the wraith back to the ceiling. Another flash of green flame, and she gagged. The air filled with the scent of rotting flesh, and now she had two wraiths to deal with.

She tried to ignore the smell threatening to choke off her air supply. As she spread her arms to aid her, she pushed power into her voice. *"Senti lesta beline soricori!"*

Two more flashes and she realized she was trapped in her attic with four wraiths.

She, their sole target.

Between the suffocating smell, the frigid cold, and the green flame that had begun licking away at her defenses, she'd had enough. The old witch infused another small amount of magic into her chanting as the dark power built around her. Pushing in at her immortal soul.

The carefully placed wards and runes began to glow around the room.

"Ah," she nodded to herself when she recognized this flavor of magic.

Death Magic.

The wielder had sent wraiths to steal her life force.

As if they had even a remote chance.

They had indeed forgotten.

Did they neglect to tell the tales of The Last Witch to their offspring? Or were they so foolish to think time and age had done anything more than strengthen her mind and magic?

Were they fooled by her decrepit body into thinking she hadn't prepared for this very moment?

She'd known all along her time on the earth wasn't done.

She'd known, and she'd spent these centuries preparing for the inevitable, forthcoming battles.

They always came.

History never failed to circle back around upon itself. Species were reliable and could be counted on to behave exactly as they had so many millennia before.

Nature, after all, was naturally predictable. It could be counted on to stay true to itself as it was designed to. Her instincts had told her to shield herself in a small old woman's body.

An appearance of weakness and fragility.

And here they were, once again, not disappointing their species and nature. She was under attack. She was ready. She never doubted for a single moment that the wars would come again. She'd made preparations.

She stood between them and the humans.

The only one left to do the hard work of protecting humankind. Not that she had any real affinity for the human species. They had, after all, destroyed her coven, killed all of her sisters and any who dared enter this world with the slightest ability to use Earth Magic the way Nature had meant for it to be used.

The current picked up around her as the green flame fought against her protection spell. The first wraith swooped dangerously close to her as the dark magic worked hard to gain the upper hand in the battle. Her long hair embraced the wind and whipped around her face and shoulders. Its force came on powerfully and threatened to knock her over. She spread her feet apart and stood steadfast, she would not waiver. She could not waiver. She was, after all, the last of the Thornwood Coven, and the last defender of humanity.

If she didn't win this one small battle, all would be lost.

Her eyes cast downward.

She shuffled her bare feet under her skirts and summoned the ancient soil from her sisters' graves. Lifting her arms above her head, she threw her head back and cast her eyes upward. Her light silver eyes glowed with magic and wisdom.

As The Last Witch's chant grew in volume, her arms grew in length and strength. The rest of her body followed suit.

Where there once stood an old woman, stooped from age, a new being emerged. She felt the power hum through her as she straightened tall to her true height, shedding her old husk and realizing her true form. She shook her head, and her hair shifted from grey and black into long strands of silver and white. Shiny, full, and lush.

She commanded her runes and pushed as much magic into them as they could bear. Now she had them. The witch threw her left arm out, and a small misshapen blue bottle flew from the tiny hidden attic cupboard and into her outstretched hand, just as the battle took a turn in her favor.

A shriek came from the ether. The glowing runes were doing their job.

Ah, too bad. Too late. No mercy would be shown this night. The Last Witch closed her fingers around the bottle that was now in her hand and, with the force of a hurricane, slammed it at her feet releasing the precious gravesite dirt. She stepped onto the ancient soil, ignoring the glass as she curled her toes into the glorious mess she'd made. Now she had them. She shifted once more, hoping to cover the exposed dirt with her long skirts, but quickly realized in her true form, her skirts no longer touched the floor.

The Last Witch smiled to herself.

"You fools! You think to attack me?" she yelled to the ceiling of the attic where the wraiths hovered.

"The time has come, crone," a disembodied voice said from a murky mass swirling on the ceiling of the attic. A ball of the green putrid flame roared at her. She flipped it away with a flick of her wrist, but the stench it left behind rocked her.

"Crone? What crone do you see?" Why did dark magic have to smell so bad, she wondered and doubled over quickly to grab handfuls of the dirt. She straightened with purpose.

"Upon my flame, I bind ye. To the wind, I cast thee. Beneath the deepest hallow, I condemn ye. Never to rise again, shall thee! Foolish foul ghoul, you are beneath me!" She threw the dirt at the darkness and blew. Her breath carried the precious soil toward the ceiling, and it burst into brilliant blue flames. Seconds later, four screaming creatures hurled themselves at the ceiling in hopes of escape.

Escape they would not find. The Last Witch pulled a long thick twig with a crystal attached from the folds of her skirt. Quickly, she pushed her magic once more in order to power the wards she'd spent several mortal lifetimes covering the inside of the attic with, and activated the runes.

She'd closed off their hopes of retreat.

No one attacked and withdrew from her. Never would she allow any being to live that attacked her, or her coven. Not man, not beast, not magical creature. Now would be no different. Sparks and smoke filled the room as the wraiths flew about in a frantic bid to survive.

The crystal at the end of her crooked stick glowed bright blue as she worked quickly to secure the attic and block any exit the wraiths might find to escape. They screamed in the agony of their defeat.

One by one, the wretched creatures fell to ashes on the old wooden floor.

She rolled her head on her neck. Fitting back into her old woman's body would take effort. It had been a century since the last time she'd allowed herself her true form.

Maybe it was time.

She looked around the destroyed room. She'd lost a full season's worth of ingredients and that was very unfortunate. Repairs would be major. Removing the stench from the attic would take a century. She'd need to find another drying chamber for her herbs.

She took a deep breath and listened as quiet washed over the old house once more. The attackers were gone, and the dark one will have to recover from her defenses. The creatures would never be available to weaponize again, and that would hurt.

Conjuring wraiths was no small feat. And four? Four was impressive. But depleting. And they would regroup. You simply didn't make a stand so boldly unless you had a long-term goal in mind.

Which meant now the foe also knew some of what she was capable of. She'd defeated four wraiths. Now they would know how strong she'd grown. What had they learned?

The witch looked around the room at the debris left behind from the battle.

She carefully retrieved several special spell containers and painstakingly gathered every speck of magical dust left behind by the intruders. She'd be able to scribe the ashes and garner some insight. How much was yet to be determined.

One thing was for sure; they'd be back.

Would she be able to hold up? Possibly, but it would be better if she wasn't alone.

It was time to summon her guardian.

Chapter 2

Cinnamon, ginger, and cloves were used to ward off evil. They are also the main ingredients of Pumpkin Spice. Beware of those who wrinkle their nose at Pumpkin Spice.

The bell over the door to the surf and bike shop rang, like it

did a hundred times a day during the summer months.
Maximillian Silverback yelled, "Be right with you," without
looking up to see who'd entered.

Crazy busy time of the year. In fact, every one of the Santa
Cruz surf shops would be slammed from now until the end of
the summer. It's when they made the money that would hold
them over throughout the short winter months. All of the
shop's water sports and leisure equipment had been rented,
and the repairs on customer owned equipment had the small
staff booked out until the end of the next month. Unless the
person who'd just entered wanted to buy a t-shirt or shorts,
they were going to be out of luck. Even as busy as they were,
the shop still had to play the game and stay open, if they

wanted to maintain a good reputation. A bad Yelp review spread quicker than wildfire, and he couldn't eat everyone who left the store unhappy. Humans tasted like dung anyway. The energy in the shop suddenly shifted. Max dropped the small motor he'd been repairing and jumped up.

"Elsie?" he asked. He knew it was her. It had to be. No one had energy as white-hot as The Last Witch.

He moved quickly from behind the counter that served as his workspace, in search of the witch who drove him out of his mind.

Could it really be her? After all this time? He didn't know if he wanted to ring her neck or hug her. Either choice could be equally deadly.

"Elsie?" he asked again, rounding the corner of a colorful surfboard display.

The sun hit him through the large plate glass window. The blinding light forced him to squint. Hesitating, his foot hung in the air, unwilling to move forward. Canine senses kicked in and the hair on the back of his neck stood straight up. He'd not survived all these centuries by ignoring his given abilities to know when he was about to step in a steaming pile of crap. On instinct, he swiftly pulled his foot back, and without making a sound, he swung on his heel and bolted out of the glass door. The bell over the door sounded alarmingly loud as it gave away his escape. He made it a scarce five feet before his store burst into dark-green flames.

The powerful explosion hit him with a force so strong, it lifted him off his feet and tossed him like a rag doll. The putrid scent of rotting flesh assaulted his senses and choked his ability to take a breath. As the asphalt rushed up to meet his face, he shifted. If Maximillian knew anything, he knew how to land. He'd been perfecting the art of landing his entire life. His feet hit the ground with a jarring force as he dropped fluidly to a crouch. Without hesitation, he sprung up and away from the tendrils of sickly green flames reaching out of the burning store toward him. The scent of the fire was like a thick sludge that coated the very air he gasped for, overwhelming his senses. He coughed and paused almost too long. A finger of the flame struck his backside and burned like acid. He twisted in pain and landed again, this time on all fours. He sprung once more, just as a wicked pair of flames stretched out for him. If the single tiny lick was any indication of the damage he'd suffer, these larger flames might cost him his life. While in the air, he placed his hand on his tattooed bicep and whispered, "*Lemme chi senti.*"

Large beautiful wings burst forth and spread wide from his sleek feathered body. With one strong flap, he caught an air current and took flight. Up and away, he soared from the flames, which continued to pursue him, screeching at the sight of his store being devoured in green dirty magic.

A dark spell.

Something was very wrong. The Last Witch would never resort to such trickery and would certainly never make an attempt against him. This, he knew, like he knew every inch of ink that covered his body. He soared over the bay and climbed a familiar cliffside as he traveled the shore on a north wind. He dove low to feel the mist of the waves crashing against the jutting rocks.

His raptor voice shrieked at the outrage of being attacked. And on two powerful thrusts from his wide wingspan, he climbed the side of the cliff inches from its face and burst forth above where the thick forest met the cliff's edge.

Another loud final screech of anger before he descended into the forest. With any luck, he'd find her. If she didn't want him to see her, he wouldn't. But if she had any inkling what was happening, or if she too, had been attacked, he might be able to locate her.

As he neared the forest floor, he used his beak and touched his shoulder, and squawked, "*Lemme chi senti.*"

Maximillian's giant clawed paws hit the ground hard, displacing twigs, leaves, and small critters. Without slowing or breaking his stride, he lumbered as quickly as his large body would allow. He knew if anyone saw an adult black bear running in the woods, they would steer clear.

She had to know he was coming. It didn't make sense to attack him before her. And anyone who'd be so bold to come for either of them had to have been in this game a very long time. This was no rookie move.

This was a declaration of war.

The large bear picked up speed. He chuffed a few times, stopped, reared back on his hind legs, and roared. Adrenaline worked through his muscles. He dropped back to all fours and pushed to move faster. He was conflicted. On the one hand, how dare a Natural come for them after all they had sacrificed only to survive. The audacity was mind-boggling.

On the other hand, it felt so good to be in motion. Even with the loss of the surf shop, the pack's only real source of income, he was alive. The energy flowing through his muscles felt good. It was about time. He shook his head because he needed this. His pack needed this.

Life had become almost unbearable. The monotony made for a bitter bedfellow. For him, for all of them.

Finally, something worth living for. Worth fighting for once more.

He felt the witch's glamour and was compelled to turn back. He knew this was the outermost section of her defense. A lesser being would have been incapacitated this close to her manor. He smiled to himself. She was going to make him work to get to her.

Good. Made things even more interesting. Some of his younger pack members didn't even know what it meant to be a wolf, much less any other creature.

The bear broke through the edge of the forest. He fought the strong desire to turn back. The witch had some serious wards in play. He was covered in her magic, and he couldn't even stand to be there.

The deadly black bear stood on its hind legs once more and roared at the field that opened up before him. He dropped down onto his front legs and made an attempt to step onto the wildflower meadow that wasn't supposed to be there. The forest surrounded the meadow, but he knew it was of her making. Somewhere out of sight was a vast manor house and estate.

Cramps gripped his stomach and nausea rolled over him. He tried to force himself to take another step, but it only resulted in him vomiting up his last meal. And the bottoms of his paws burned like they'd been dipped in acid.

He swiped his paw across his muzzle and roared again. The pain was unbearable, even for a bear.

His chest seized, and he fell to his side. He had no strength left. He couldn't even hold his form. She was going to kill him.

"Maximillian Silverback. Do you have a death wish?"

The naked man rolled to his back and flung his arms out to either side. Too weak to do anything more than grimace.

"Witch."

"Wolf."

He watched her step forward. Her white silver hair was in hundreds of braids, with bits of metal woven throughout that glinted and glimmered in the sunlight. The long braids were pulled back into a massive sweep that tumbled about her shoulders and down her back. Black eyebrows and thick black lashes served to enhance her otherworldly, silver cat-eyes. She wore a soft, black, sleeveless tunic over bare legs. Black clogs covered her toes and left her ankles and heels exposed. She was lean, tan, and muscular. She'd also draped her neck and wrists in crystals and rune stones.

"This is the image you give me after all these years?" He smiled, wondering why she hid the runes that covered her body. She'd always been a beautiful witch. Her independence and integrity only enhanced her lovely attributes. One thing he knew, she hadn't welcomed him yet and that gave him a moment of pause.

She cocked her head and watched him.

He smiled again. He'd forgotten how fun it was to walk on the wild side. He missed living a dangerous life. Witches weren't known for their sense of humor after all.

"Is there another version of me you prefer, guardian?" she asked and tilted her head in the opposite direction.

"My shop was attacked by vile magic," he snarled. The pain in his stomach increased, and his knees jack-knifed to his chest. His heart pounded so hard and loud he thought for sure it was going to land on the ground in front of him, and he broke out in a sweat.

The witch flipped her wrist, and the pressure in his stomach, chest and subsequent pain in his body disappeared.

Maximillian relaxed his midsection with a groan. He brought his arms up and studied his hands for blisters. Just as he thought; no damage.

He rolled over to his hands and knees as he no longer found comfort laying belly exposed on the ground looking up at the witch.

"What did the magic look like?" she asked as he climbed to his feet and stood to tower over her. She did not, he noted, move back.

"Green flame devoured my shop. Disgusting smelly green magic that reached for me even after I escaped the building." He spit on the ground. "It stunk of rotting flesh."

"Were you injured?" she asked.

Maximillian twisted to view his backside. Since the healing mark was placed upon his body, injuries disappeared as if they had never existed during the change from human to creature and back. He never took it for granted and always wondered if it would cease to work one day. Of course, as long as she lived, and his markings were never altered, they would remain as trustworthy as she was. Even centuries later her magic impressed him.

"You look like you made it out okay." She looked him up and down.

He looked at himself and smirked. The Witch rolled her eyes and flicked her wrist once more, and Max found himself in loose-fitting dark grey trousers, with a black button-up shirt.

"Nice." Max smiled arrogantly. "I clean up well, don't I?

She took in his broad shoulders, thick thighs, and shoulder-length dark brown hair that matched his scruffy beard, and something stirred inside her. She'd missed this damn wolf more than she'd have liked or was ever going to admit.

"Your appearance was never a problem," the Last Witch muttered.

The shifter looked his Witch up and down. "Neither was yours. Hug?"

She hissed and pulled back. "Why would you need a hug, Wolf?"

"I've been attacked. My surf shop destroyed. I might be feeling some kind of way about it."

"The elation of the battles to come is rolling off of you like bad cologne."

He smirked again. She could always read him. It's why he never got away with anything.

"Whoever the magic maker was, they used your white light to draw me in. I could have sworn it was you."

"Me, you say?"

"Yes, whoever it was came swift and sure. They knew who and what I am. I'm sure of it."

"Tell me about the fire."

"It was an explosion really. The green flame only appeared after I'd fled and was thrown several feet."

She swiveled her gaze back to him. With a furrowed brow, she asked, "How did you escape the green flame?"

"Listened to my instincts."

"They will never fail you."

"So you've said a million times."

The Witch nodded. "I'm glad to hear something managed to sink in." She rolled her eyes. "I was going to summon you and your wolves anyway."

"You were? Why?"

"It's time, Maximillian." She turned and walked across the field toward the manor house that was becoming clearer as her magic allowed it to morph into view.

"What's changed?" he asked, and then his gaze found the sight he'd been eager to behold. His shoulders relaxed. "There it is. Paradise."

Maximillian Silverback followed his charge with renewed vigor in his step. Energy pulsing through his veins that he hadn't felt for three centuries.

The magic veil lifted fully, and the home he knew almost as well as he'd known his own, appeared before him.

Thornwood Manor. It seemed larger than before. Of course, it had been almost three centuries since he'd set foot in it. Knowing the Witch, much would have changed since his last visit.

The old Victorian Gothic structure loomed ahead. With its dark wood accents and pointed rooflines, it was straight out of the horror movies the wolflings liked so much. Black forged iron gates attached to large block pillars surrounded the grounds. A smaller version of the gates sectioned off the Witch's various gardens that were scattered around the estate property.

He knew one thing, and that was you stayed out of this Witch's gardens. As that last thought ran through his mind, his eyes landed on one garden gate that had a larger entrance than the rest, a tall iron fence with various creatures' skulls on the peaks around it, and real skull and crossbones hung across the entrance.

"Still maintaining the Garden of Death, eh?" He stopped and studied the plot of land in question. The back of the vast rows of planting beds met up against a large pond and a small hill just at the edge of the forest. He spied the miniature huts and homes that littered the hill and smiled.

"Good to see there are other Naturals here still living and breathing."

"And working." The Last Witch stopped walking, nodded toward the garden, and said, "these are the last of their kind on earth. When these few vanish, their species will be gone from the mortal realm, once and for all."

"Terrible times we've come to see, Witch."

"Indeed, Wolf. Indeed."

"You offer them protection?" Maximillian asked.

She nodded. "They tend to the Death Garden, and I provide a safe home for them and their offspring. It's a fair trade."

He watched the small fairy village for a few moments. It was hard to believe this was the last of its kind in existence. At one time, the small wood fairy was so plentiful they bordered on pest status. Now, only one tiny village remained.

A small waterfall fed the large pond, trickling down the face of the hill. The small stone and wood homes lined either side of the waterfall and along the pond's edge. They'd rigged up some kind of irrigation system with twigs and leaves. A decent size water wheel was in operation, and smaller windmills sat on the hill behind the homes. They might be the last of their kind, but no one could say they weren't an industrious lot.

"I'd forgotten how beautiful their wings are as they flit about," he muttered, mesmerized by their activity as they flitted about.

"I need to show you something," the Last Witch said.

The pair continued their walk toward Thornwood Manor. Max spotted large black weather vanes that were forged in the same heavy ornate iron as the gates. One for each pointed octagon-shaped tower. Each tower had at least one ornate window with heavily framed colored glass. The highest tower looked as if it had taken damage. The roofline had a tree branch hanging from it, and there was a huge gaping hole where the window had once sat.

"Looks like Thornwood is in need of repair," he said and nodded toward the damaged fourth-story room.

She shrugged her shoulders and didn't respond.

He looked to his feet. "The matching slate cobblestone and slate roof shingles are nice. New?"

"If any time within the last seventy-five years is considered new, then yes." She led him to the wraparound porch. Each room on the first floor had a glass door. The ability to escape or enter and see what you were entering to or leaving from.

"You've replaced the wood shingles on the side of the manor with mud?" he asked, noting the modern silver sage stucco that now acted as the exterior.

"With the fires in the mountains becoming more and more dangerous, I chose to utilize many modern conveniences."

"Your Magic doesn't hold back the fires?"

"Don't be a fool. Of course it does. But I like the cool feel of the plaster and the attractive color it adds."

"You embedded wards in the stucco, didn't you?"

She smiled. "Wards, runes, and banishment jars, along with all sorts of delightful surprises to anyone who'd think to move against this house and its occupants."

Chills ran over his skin.

"Foreboding is heavy, Witch."

"I've felt it too. I've been preparing the manor for the coven to return. They won't know how to use their magic as one until all thirteen are awake and sharing the same space. That alone will be a feat."

"It's time, then?" he asked.

"Guardian, it's well past time, I fear."

"Where do you plan to put them? So much magic concentrated in beings who have no idea how to control it will be a tough transition. For you and them."

"I've prepared their sleeping quarters already. Two to a room, I'm afraid." She looked to the heavens and closed her eyes. "The real challenge will be getting the entire Thirteen to the manor alive. I fear we may be too late."

More chills ran over his skin, and his gaze turned back to the manor house he'd once called home.

A heavy, blackwood trimmed the corners, windows, and doorways. Large black wood columns held up the roof of the porch on which pots hung of every shape and size, stuffed full of various overgrown plants.

Giant blue and green pots lined the slate steps to the porch. Max eyed the mismatched pots. Anything could be growing in them with this Witch as the gardener. He'd learned his lesson in the 1600s when he'd mistakenly smelled the wrong blooming flower and spent the next several months as a blue jay, unable to transform. Staying away from household cats had become a life-or-death situation.

He shivered. Everything the eye could see was placed there for a purpose. Every decoration only served as a ward or rune. The more misshapen the appearance, the surer you could be that magic was afoot.

He followed her up the short flight of wide steps and across the porch to the ornately carved front door.

"I've something you need to see," she said, placing her hand on the knob.

"So you say. Get on with it, then." Max was sure whatever it was would be the thing that had brought him to her.

"I caught one," the Last Witch said and opened the heavy door. The hair on the back of his neck stood up again.

"One what?" The Last Witch smiled knowingly and Max's stomach turned. What had she done?

Chapter 3

Plant lavender by your gate for good luck.

"It needs to be banished!" Maximillian shouted.

"I will banish it once I've learned all I can from it," the Last Witch shouted back and ducked. The wraith was desperate to escape the chamber the Witch had locked the three of them in. Its form didn't allow it the ability to unlock or open doors, but even if it did, it was no match for the Witch, or for that matter; the Wolf.

That knowledge didn't stop it from following its nature to survive and maintain its futile attempts to escape. It thrashed its spectral body against the doors and window, again and again. When the wraith finally realized it had no way out, it turned its attention to the other beings in the chamber. Namely, the Witch it was sent to destroy and her guardian.

"You were attacked too?" Max dodged the wraith and watched it circle the room.

"Yes, last night." The witch remained as still as possible without taking her eyes off of it.

"Why didn't you summon me?" he asked as took her by the shoulders and moved her a step to her left just as the wraith buzzed the twosome.

"I took care of it," she replied while continuing to study the deadly creature.

The wraith sent out an unearthly screech as a warning just before the air turned frigid. It watched the Witch while keeping tabs on the Wolf who was in perpetual motion. Unlike the Witch who stood so still the wraith couldn't tell if she was breathing except for the little puffs of cold breath that left her mouth when she exhaled.

"Here we go," the Witch whispered. Without taking her eyes from the wraith, she took a crystal pendant that was hanging from around her neck and held it up.

"What do you see?" Maximillian whispered, without taking his eyes from the wraith.

The Witch adjusted the pendant to peer through it from a different angle.

"I can't quite grab its magical signature," she whispered back. "Its creator has shielded itself well."

"How did you capture it?"

"Well, truthfully, I sort of killed it and brought it back."

Maximillian stepped back on a hiss. "*Necromancy!*"

"Oh, stop it. I didn't use *Death Magic*." She turned a bone-chilling gaze toward the Wolf. "It was never alive, you fool. It's a conjured beastie and therefore never truly had a life. I simply re-conjured it." She shook her head and returned to her study of the creature hovering near the domed ceiling. "Unfortunately, when I re-conjured it, I was forced to add too much of my own magic and now the original magic maker's signature is diluted even more." She elbowed Max. "Rile it up again. I can't see any magic but my own when it's calm."

"Rile it up? How do you propose I do that?" Max placed his hands on his hips.

She shrugged. "Fight it."

"Fight it? You want me to fight it for you?"

The Witch looked at the Wolf. "You're my guardian, aren't you? I need you to fight the thing for me." She gestured toward the wraith. "Fight it."

"I only fight to protect you," he growled, and then mumbled, "even if you haven't needed a protector for a long time. You didn't even summon me when you were attacked."

Her gaze remained on him. "I know you're unhappy with me. But you are my sworn guardian, and I am asking you to fight the wraith so I can learn who attacked us."

"You know I'm unhappy with you? How could you possibly know that? On top of not summoning your only protector, you've had nothing to do with me for centuries," he shouted.

"I was busy." The Witch returned to viewing the wraith through her crystal pendant.

"Do you have any idea what a sworn guardian goes through when his witch won't let him near her?" He turned his broad shoulders to face her. "I haven't seen you with my own eyes for almost two hundred years. Do you even care how excruciatingly boring life becomes for a witchless wolf?"

"Boring?" the Witch hissed and turned her focus back to Max. "I am the last of my kind. The only one left in existence. I gave you the option of severing our bond, and you refused. I made provisions and allowances for your wolves that would have been blasphemous at any other time in our history. I've spent the last three hundred years here while my coven sisters have been locked in their death slumber, preparing for the battle that is now upon us. You did, what? Sat in your surf shop, rutted with the young human tourists, and drank all night... every night."

She rolled her eyes. "Meanwhile, I'm trying to figure out if the souls of my sisters survived, and if the awakening spell I've created will bring them back to me once they're here. Or," she took her eyes from the creature sent to kill her in her own home and glared at the most infuriating wolf she'd ever known, "if the magic we worked so many centuries ago didn't hold at all... and you're complaining of boredom?" Her cat-like eyes transitioned from their normal glowing silver to a bright white.

The temperature in the chamber grew cold once more. The wraith became agitated again and circled the ceiling of the domed octagon-shaped room.

Maximillian folded his arms across his chest, "I could have helped you prepare; you know. I'm an unmatched *valoir*."

"Max, you know, and I know you know because I explained it a million times, I couldn't allow myself the luxury of your company while my sisters and their own guardians suffered."

"The coven made the right decision. The guardian mates agreed."

"Then you understand."

"No, I don't understand how making us suffer made it better for them. Even now you hide your runes from me."

She turned and studied her guardian and for the first time saw the true level of damage she'd inflicted to their bond by locking herself away from him. He'd never trust her again, at worst. It would take her centuries to earn his trust back, at best.

"You weren't on the verge of becoming an extinct species." The Witch looked back through her crystal and said with a deep sigh, "I have no appetite for the past. But it seems to haunt me at every turn."

She waved her hand and whispered, *"See me."*

The glow covering her smooth tan skin faded, and her black as midnight tattoos became visible. She had centuries of protection spells permanently guarding her body. There were enhancement runes across her forehead showcased in the moon phases, a brilliant glowing star at her third eye, and focusing marks on the top of her cheekbones. He lost count of all the newly added marks.

"Does this suit?" she asked.

His eyes roamed the exposed parts of her arms and then met hers. "You've added so many," he whispered.

"I have several I want to add to your body too. I'm stronger than I was the last time we were together. I know more." She leaned toward him. "My *maginka* is much more powerful. I should go over some of your older markings. Make sure you have the best I can offer you." She straightened and watched him from the corner of her eye.

Max studied her closely and realized the Witch he once knew was gone. This was a new version of her, and he would be smart to remember that.

"It is my honor to receive whatever you wish to mark my body with." He turned his focus back to the creature at hand. "Whenever you like."

He'd be there to enforce her wishes and make sure she stayed alive. It was the least he could do. And in the meantime, he'd figure out what else she needed from him. Hopefully, whatever it was would be something he could deliver.

The witch refocused and peered intently through her pendant at the wraith, whispering, "*Unveil your magis.*" The power of her words bounced off the walls of the chamber like several echoes, each one sounding a second or two behind the other until they became nothing more than a whisper.

The wraith let out another ethereal screech and dove for the two. The Wolf crouched behind the Witch and prepared for the attack. The Witch stood motionless and studied the conjured creature through her crystal as it headed toward her. Moments before the wraith's attack on the Witch was certain, the Wolf stood to his impressive height behind her. He positioned his arms over her head, tapped the inside of his wrists together, and shouted, "*Lemme vast tect.*"

A white light of protection appeared around the couple, and the wraith disintegrated the second it impacted Max's magic.

"Dammit, Elsie!" Max yelled, dropping his arms, and his protection. He wasn't sure if he was mad or excited. Possibly equal measures of both. "You need to be more careful."

"Thank you," she said, ignoring his outburst. "However, I was unable to solidly identify the wraith's *magis*. I felt magic I hadn't felt in centuries. But how can it be? It can't be so." She shook her head. "That magic has been dead since before we migrated from Europe."

"Who?"

"I'm hesitant to say who, exactly, but I can say what."

"What, then? What are we preparing to go to war with?"

"Death Magic, I'm afraid."

"I hate Death Magic and everything associated with it." Max's large body shivered.

"Yes, well, while you were surfing and consuming, I was preparing. Not specifically for that particular foe, but in general. I knew the next war would be with a faction of the Naturals."

"The humans couldn't care less about magic and its makers."

"'Tis the only reason we're safe from them."

"Will Vampire have influence like they did in the past?"

"They may, but the human population is so great, they have nothing to fear from us. No, this war is the last one between the Naturals who are left...and me. It will determine who lives and who vanishes completely."

"What is the prize?"

"The Earth. Humanity is destroying it. The Vampire don't care, because they can live anywhere humans thrive. It's the Naturals who will fight to limit the humans and their staggering numbers."

"Too many humans."

"Indeed, Wolf."

"Whose side do we sit on?"

"We sit on our own side. The humans don't need us any longer. After their treachery, I'd not lay down my life, or any others, for them again."

"What do we fight for, then?"

"It's not what we fight *for*, my Maximillian. It's what we fight *against*. Death Magic."

He nodded. He understood the impact unchecked Death Magic had on all living beings.

"If the green flame is any indication of the wielder's power, we won't be able to do it alone."

"Exactly my thought."

"Then it's true? What you said? It's time to bring them home?"

"Yes, Max. It's time." She turned to face her guardian. "We need to add at least one new mark. One of protection."

"Like I said, anytime you want. But you've placed so many on me already. Is this for me or you? Do you think you're going to be harder to keep safe?"

"I think all of the guardians need to be marked with a protection rune against Death Magic. Just in case. For themselves and the witches they guard. I spent years developing the spell. Almost as an afterthought. I never dreamed it would be called into service so soon."

"I'll need to gather my wolves. Most don't even know what it means to be a guardian. Some may not desire the connection the bond brings after observing me."

Elsie thought about that. "Do any of the coven's original guardians still live?"

"The only one who stayed close by is Alicastor Blue. The rest scattered after the first hundred years, and one by one, they've stopped checking in over the decades since."

"Oh."

Elsie was devastated to hear the Wolf shifters had suffered so. They'd always been the perfect companion for Witches. It was becoming even more clear to Elsie no matter how hard she tried to protect those she cared for, she always seemed to fall short.

"How many are here now?" she asked.

"I have a pack of roughly thirty wolves and three wolflings. Only one was a guardian, and only five are old enough to remember when witches walked the earth." Max rolled his dark eyes over to her.

"So few," she whispered. "Will the original wolves help the younger ones? How many of the pack do you think will be up for the war ahead?"

"All."

"All?"

"I wasn't kidding when I said it has been sheer boredom. We're wolves. Made for protecting, fighting, mating, and hunting. Not made for laying around, getting fat and playing video games all day. Even with the surfing, it's been brutal. Horrible for the wolflings. Some days I can't get them out of the house and into the woods."

Elsie couldn't hold back the bark of laughter. She'd missed the wolves but especially this one. The one male she'd always been able to count on. The only species that the witches could know for certain wouldn't turn on them. In fact, the past proved they would lay down their lives for her or any of her coven sisters without hesitation.

Loyalty. Such a powerfully misused word. Most people who saw themselves as loyal had only an inkling of what that truly meant.

"We need to make sure they all know what they're getting into," she said.

"I don't think we have a choice. They've attacked my shop and specifically targeted me. We have to assume it's because I stand between them and you. It has to be someone who has a vast knowledge of you, us, the agreement."

"If that's the case your Wolves aren't safe, either. You'll need to get them here. We'll make lodging for them. Then the first order of business is seeing who is willing to be dispatched. As the coven's magic awakens, but before they become aware...it'll be an exceptionally dangerous time. If we are correct and this is an old foe, the sisters are in grave danger. If only one of them is removed or doesn't regain her magic... we all fall... and we, along with humanity, will be in grave peril."

"Do you plan to rescind the slumber spell all at once or one at a time?"

"One at a time. It's the only way we can dispatch the wolves who wish to become guardians. If we recall the spell all at once, the coven will light up like a magical map, and magic makers with the smallest amount of credibility would be able to locate them. One at a time affords us the ability to control her awakening. And security."

"I'll summon my wolves." Max turned on his heel and left the chamber.

Once outside, he looked to the sky. He loved the atmosphere of Thornwood Manor and its grounds. This was a pivotal moment. He placed his hands on his hips and dug his toes into the loose dirt. He could feel the energy coming from the earth. Change was afoot. Big change.

He took in the overflowing gardens and the busy fairies. The pond, its waterfall, and the water wheel as it spun. He mused as a fight between two wood fairies broke out near the small windmills scattered on the hill just beyond the pond. As he watched the small child fairies dipped their wings in and out of the fall and wondered if this little slice of magical paradise would look the same once whatever was to come ...came. He doubted it. You simply didn't live as long as he did and not know with every fiber of your being how even the smallest ripple can make the largest impact. And thus far, this was not small.

These attacks were declarations of war. The 'who' of it all was the only real question. The 'why' could be assumed. But until the 'who' was identified, the 'why' would make them insane.

Elsie stepped up behind him. In centuries past, she would have wrapped her arms around his midsection and lay her head on his back. The countless memories of her performing that simple show of affection almost brought him to his knees. She hesitated behind him. He knew he wasn't making it easy for her, but the years apart hadn't been easy for him. She needed to know what it cost him.

"You're different, you know," she said quietly.

"We're all different, Elsie."

"I fear the time I have left here is coming to an end." She wrapped her arms around his stomach like so many times before, and he released the breath he'd been holding.

"The need to establish a new coven before I'm gone drives me now harder than ever before," she whispered and laid her head against his broad back.

"Did you see your end, then?" he asked and turned to face her, dislodging her embrace.

"Not exactly, but I know I am not long for this earth. I need to do this last big thing before I move on." She shrugged her shoulders and took a step back. "There is much to do and we have little time. The enemy found both of us easily enough. If any of the coven members come back into the smallest level of their magic before their ritual, they will be unprotected and vulnerable."

"Let's make sure that doesn't happen. You want the Wolves here? You're sure?" He searched her face.

She nodded. "We must band together like never before, if we are to see the end of this."

"I'll be back before nightfall." Max made a move to touch his chest tattoo when Elsie placed her hand gently on his bicep. He looked down at her.

"When this is done, I'll give you your freedom."

"When this is done, you'll try." He touched his bicep and muttered, "*Lemme chi senti.*"

The Last Witch watched as the guardian who had sworn to protect her a millennia ago took flight as a majestic bird of prey.

She shivered. The foreboding was strong.

Time to prepare Thornwood Manor for the battle to come.

Chapter 4

Keep aloe growing in your home to heal burns and welcome good fortune.

The giant snake slithered over my skin and coiled around

my body. I tried to kick it away, but it held firm. The creature wrapped itself around my legs and midsection, working its way up to my chest. I struggled to take a breath, but the pressure only increased. Panic spread throughout my body as the struggle intensified.

Darkness closed in, and no matter which way I turned, I couldn't find a path to the light. This thing was going to kill me if I didn't break free. I twisted hard in an attempt to loosen the vice-like grip. I opened my mouth to scream, but no sound came forth.

Sweat dripped from my exhausted body. With one final push, I gave it everything I had left in me, and flipped myself to my back.

I awoke when a roaring boom shook my building. I sat up in my bed, panting like I'd been fighting for my life.

A dream.

It was just a dream. No. It was more than a dream. It was a nightmare. Not just any ol' nightmare, but an honest to God night terror. My head was pounding, and my body felt feverish.

I blinked at the darkness and tried to grab hold of reality. It didn't help. In fact, it only made matters worse. I knew my bedroom like the back of my hand, but everything seemed...wrong.

Off, like it was all my stuff, but... wasn't. I felt disconnected and I didn't like it.

"Come on, Cassandra, it was just a bad dream." That's me, Cassandra Backman, talking to myself again. I'm an artist and a bit of a loner. My condo was my salvation, and I mostly worked alone, although I did have a couple of artist friends with whom I collaborated with on projects. My severe diabetes kept me from going out to eat or drink with friends, so I didn't have many. Some days, if I didn't talk to me, no one would.

Lightning struck somewhere close, and my room lit up. For a moment, I swore I saw movement near my dresser. The tips of my fingers tingled. I tried to run my hands through my tangled hair and stopped short when I realized I was drenched in sweat.

I nearly jumped out of my skin when thunder boomed close by and my window rattled.

I let my head drop and reached for the dream but couldn't quite grab it. Whatever I'd dreamed this time had left a residue of fear and pain through my weak and trembling limbs. It was so hard for me to shake off the night terrors.

I heard an odd sound and froze, straining to listen. I couldn't tell if it was coming from the inside of my sweet, little one-bedroom condo I'd scrimped and saved to purchase last year. My condo was located on the second floor, so burglary wasn't something I worried too much about, but you never knew these days what lengths people would go to get what they wanted. I knew that better than anyone.

Lightning flashed again outside my bedroom window, followed by a low rumble of thunder. I took a deep breath and held it, listening. I soon realized the sound I'd heard was my own heartbeat loud inside my chest.

Another flash came again, brightening up my dark room like a strobe light. Seconds later, as if on cue, my bedroom was drenched in darkness, and thunder shook my building. Summer storms were unusual for Sacramento, California, but not impossible.

The sweat-soaked tank top stuck to my skin and felt gross. Panic was setting in. I needed to wake my hands up. The tingling was getting worse the more awake I became, which was the opposite of what it should have been. My blood sugar levels must be majorly off. Losing appendages was a constant worry when you had the type of diabetes I had. Most people who suffered from the same affliction as me could expect to lose a finger or two, if not a leg.

A tree branch scraped my window, sending shivers over my skin.

Cool water would feel great on my face. A few splashes and I might be able to get back to sleep. I had a big day ahead, and I couldn't afford not to be well-rested and alert in the morning. I leapt from my bed in the general direction of my en-suite bathroom, like I had a million times before. Except this time, I fell, arms sprawled out flat on my face in the middle of my floor. The thrashing about in bed had caused me to tangle myself up in my sheets, and my legs were twisted and bound together. The harder I tried to disengage from them, the tighter they seemed to wrap around my limbs.

"Aarrggghhhh," I yelled out in frustration and flipped myself over into a sitting position so I could see the sheets that had assaulted my legs.

"Let. Me. Go," I growled at them, and they obeyed. I laughed at the absurdity of it all and disengaged from the clingy fabric. Leaving the chaotic sheets piled on the bedroom floor, I padded to my bathroom.

I shivered as the storm continued to rage outside.

My heart was pounding in my chest, only now it was quick and loud versus just being loud. Between the bad dream, the storm, and now the bedsheet trying to kill me, I was wide awake, with little chance of getting back to sleep.

I located my blood testing kit and did a quick jab at the tip of my tingling finger to see if my sugars were off. It was the only thing I knew that would make my fingers feel like this. I must be very out of sync. I'd never felt this intensity of discomfort before. Great, this meant more lab tests and co-pays for tests I couldn't afford.

I waited a few seconds for the result and was surprised to see my sugar level was better than it had ever been upon waking. I didn't trust it. I'd need to keep a close eye on my blood today. I gave myself a jab of long-lasting insulin and reached into the shower to flip on the hot water. Washing the sweat off my body might let me relax back to sleep. One could hope, anyway.

While the shower was warming, I took care of business and went to the sink to wash my hands. The hot running water in the shower caused the mirror to fog up. I used my middle finger to trace a straight vertical line with a swish and a squiggly horizontal line running across it. The symbol had been showing up in my art since puberty, and any time I was upset or things weren't going my way, the symbol seemed to calm me. I chalked it up to my creative brain working just a little bit differently than normal people's brains. I made a couple of smaller versions of the larger lines on the mirror and then used the palm of my hand to wipe it away, exposing my reflection.

I studied myself in the mirror. My long copper-colored hair with light blonde ends was matted and stuck to my face. I leaned in closer. Usually, the tips held a golden hue. No matter what color I dyed my hair, it always faded back to the light gold overnight. When I cut my hair, the gold came back within a day. But now my hair was brighter, and my ends had an almost white metallic quality to them. It was so shiny; it didn't look real.

Great. My hair was doing weird stuff again. It wasn't fair. No one else I knew had to deal with their hair deciding what color it wanted to be and staying that way, regardless of what I did. Blowouts; Japanese and Brazilian, foils, cuts, highlights, low lights, ... I've tried it all, none of it worked on my weird as heck hair. It always went back to copper with light gold ends... that were now white... and were my annoying ends now glowing?

Shaking my head, I twisted my hair up to form a messy bun and twisted it a little harder so it would stay in place. I leaned down to splash my face and thrust my cupped hands under the running water.

As soon as my hands hit the water a giant plume of steam blew up in my face. I immediately jumped back.

"Oh, poop!"

I stumbled on my shower mat, tripped on my own two feet, and landed on my butt. I sat there for a second attempting to recover. What a crazy night! Just what I didn't need. First the night terror, then my sheet tried to kill me, and now my plumbing was out too. I scrambled to my feet, turned the shower off, and grabbed the back scrubber hanging from my shower head. I used the handle to flip the lever to the off position on my sink.

My shoulders relaxed a little as soon as the water stopped flowing from the faucet.

Giving the bathroom sink a wide berth, I left the small room and made my way to my kitchen. A broken water whatever was going to cost me a pretty penny to have repaired. It had to. Nothing was cheap and everything cost a small fortune to fix on the condo. As much as I wanted to own my own home, keeping everything repaired and up to date was costly. I didn't know how people managed the larger homes I worked in.

I kicked at the offending sheets as I walked past them from the bathroom, and glanced at the macabre scene that was my bed. I realized the tangled sheet that tried to kill me was halfway across the room from where the sheet should have been.

Lightning strobed in my room again, enhancing the dark sweat marks caused by the night terror I couldn't remember. Another flash of lightning and the low rumble of thunder brought forth a serious war zone vibe. Pillows were rumpled and in disarray, my quilt was bunched up and half hanging off the bed, and the fitted sheet was off on one corner.

"Fix yourself!" I growled at my bed and stomped the rest of the way through my bedroom to the kitchen.

Once there, I threw open my refrigerator doorway more aggressively than it deserved and stared blankly. Nothing appealed to me. I had this weird feeling that I was supposed to remember something. For the life of me, I couldn't quite recall it.

I'd also forgotten why I'd come into the kitchen.

I glanced at the sink. Oh yeah. Maybe the plumbing issue was isolated to the bathroom. I really didn't want to have plumbing problems. I couldn't afford an unexpected bill.

Keeping a close eye on my kitchen sink, I closed the refrigerator door and found my broom. Carefully, I used the handle to move the faucet in the on position. I watched as water ran freely from the faucet into the sink with no puffs of steam. My shoulders relaxed, and I exhaled a deep breath. I put the broom away and wiggled my fingers. The tips weren't tingling anymore. The insulin must be kicking in. I was still apprehensive about sticking my hands in the water, just in case the plumbing problem had found its way to the kitchen. I found a clean washcloth and set it in the sink to wet it and turned the water off. Carefully, I picked the washcloth up and wiped off my face and hands. I spent the next few minutes at my kitchen sink doing the best job I could of cleaning myself of the sweat from the bad dream.

I realized since I'd left the bedroom, I hadn't heard any more lightning. The storm seemed to be quieting too. I relaxed a little more but still felt a low hum in my body that wasn't going away until I figured out what the dream was about. I looked around my small kitchen, decided a cup of tea was in order, and set about heating the water.

Well, it was certain I wouldn't be able to get back to sleep now. I might as well get some quotes and invoices typed up and off to my customers. I needed to keep the money flowing in. At least I was making the most of my awake time. The job I was starting later that morning was going to be stressful. Everything had to look like it was moving smoothly. It would either make or break me. Everyone knew bad word-of-mouth spread quicker than anything good. It was just the way of my world as a decorative painter.

I spent the next couple of hours on my admin work, and once I had everything I needed to send out via email, I sat back in the small chair I had paired with a cute little desk. I didn't need much, so the small duo, along with a little half filing cabinet, worked perfectly. They had all three been cast-offs that I'd picked up for free at various times. Once I'd worked my magic on them, they were gorgeous. I'd made a few basic repairs, gone with a soft blue watercolor vibe, accented in bright pink and yellow flowers, and then washed the whole set in a pearly white. Once that was complete, I'd trimmed them with rose gold and then hit the edges with a sanding block. The finish was incredible. It was a fancy feminine look with a touch of distress and gave off a beachy vibe.

My living room was small, so I didn't want anything that would overpower the rest of my furnishings. I kept it simple, with a white loveseat and chair that had every shape and color of throw pillows on them I could find. My coffee and end tables were also freebies I'd rescued and reclaimed. They were finished in white, and then I'd applied silver leaf for a distressed mirror finish that worked regardless of what colors I decorated with. I'd used the same white and silver finish on the wall that framed the only window in the room. It brightened the small dark space and made it seem larger than it was.

I had a small breakfast bar that opened the kitchen up to the living room. The two small bar stools had the same white and silver finish. The seats on the stools I'd covered in an abstract multi-color print that spoke beautifully to my throw pillows. I had a large silver framed mirror over my couch that helped enlarge the appearance of the room and several small mismatched silver mirrors surrounding the larger one. My little condo reflected my personality to a T, and I loved how I'd transformed the sparse surroundings into a shabby chic feminine paradise.

Now I just needed everything not to break on me so I could replenish my finances from purchasing the place. If I had to keep spending my money on repairs, I was never going to get caught up.

This next job would help. It was a very public building I was working in, and if it went well, I'd get more work than I'd be able to handle and that would be a game-changer for my micro business, Color by Cassie. Even if the person who I reported to was a shrew, I would get some crazy exposure, and it was worth putting up with her.

I closed out browser tabs and shut down my computer. At least I was a little ahead of the game on my paperwork. I hated paperwork, but without it, I didn't get paid. I usually put it off until the very last minute, so getting it caught up before it was even due felt fantastic. It almost wiped away the nervous energy the nightmare had caused.

I glanced to my lone window and saw the morning light peeking through my white floor-length curtains. I stretched into a standing position and located my yoga mat next to my couch. I needed to be in good shape, and since my sleep had been disturbed, a nice yoga workout before heading to work might balance the day for me.

One could hope, anyway.

Through my down dogs and cat cows, something kept me distracted. There was a memory or thought I felt compelled to pull up, but it remained just out of reach.

This was going to drive me nuts. I finished the yoga, rolled up my mat, and for once was happy I took my shower at night when I got home from work. I really didn't have it in me to deal with the bad bathroom plumbing, but would need to figure something out.

I grabbed my toothbrush and the little makeup I wore from my bathroom and went back to the kitchen sink to prepare for the day. While brushing my teeth, I made a mental note to call a plumber and then chuckled to myself 'cuz I knew my mental notes were crap, at best. Give me a color formula, and I'd remember it till my deathbed, but everyday things I needed to keep me alive were frequently elusive. I told people it was my creative brain. I hoped that was true. Lord knows it has cost me.

I was a single gal because I couldn't remember dates, events, or birthdays. But I'd also found a way to make money with my weird brain and that wasn't nothing.

My foster parents told me I would amount to nothing and not to come crawling back to them when I couldn't make it. They were the fifth foster family I'd lived with during my childhood, and nowhere near the worst. They probably weren't wrong that I would have done better financially by accepting the scholarship to law school, but just because I can test well in an area, doesn't mean I would be good at it or would have any desire to do the work.

Then they tried to force me to join the military. Luckily for me, the military wanted no part of a young artist type with severe diabetes. I had no memory of my parents and honestly had no idea what had happened to them. All I knew was that

I'd been a ward of the state since infanthood. I hadn't spoken to my foster parents in fifteen years when the Christmas card I sent them came back undeliverable.

By the time I needed to get dressed for work, the sun was fully up and streaming into my bedroom. I went to the only other window in my condo and slid the curtains open. The after-storm light was bright and felt wonderful on my face. I took a moment to appreciate it.

I grabbed my overalls and t-shirt and dressed in my painter's uniform as efficiently as I could. My boots weren't where I usually left them, so a frantic search ensued around my bedroom. Dropping down to my hands and knees at the foot of my bed, I lifted the bed skirt and comforter.

"There you are, you little buggers."

I found them, tucked neatly under my bed right where I'd taken them off the previous night before my shower. I grabbed the boots, dropped the bed skirt, and popped up to sit on my bed to pull them on.

Something was off, but I couldn't quite place it. The bed looked fine. I'd done a great job making it. Better than I'd done in a while.

Wait, when did I make my bed? That was weird. Well, no need to worry about it. It wasn't like bed fairies slipped in while I was working to make my bed. I must have done it and forgotten. That was the problem with a blood sugar condition. It often wreaked havoc in the oddest way.

I located my phone and found the medical app for my insurance. Shooting a quick email off to my overworked doctor had me feeling a little better. The new diabetic meds might be causing some unusual side effects. Although my tests had been good, it was better to get it checked out. I'd rather be safe than sorry.

Once done, I stood, placed my hands on my hips, and surveyed the immaculately made bed. It must have been the best-made bed I'd ever seen.

"This is going to be a very long day."

Chapter 5

I made my way out of my condo and to my SUV to get her running. She was an old girl and needed time to warm-up her moving parts and get her fluids flowing before I expected her to haul me and my equipment around town. I understood this and tried to give her all the time she needed to prepare for the day.

While I waited for her to do her thing, I opened the roll-up door to my garage. It was one of the reasons I'd chosen this condo. It came with its own one and a half car garage along with a parking space. I used the parking space to park Ol' Bessie, my beater SUV, and the garage was my workspace slash warehouse. I backed Ol' Bessie up to the garage door and loaded into her the plaster, tools, and other items I'd need before I started the task of securing my ladder and scaffolding to the top of my vehicle.

I was finishing up, had my rear passenger door open, was standing on the running board to gain the height I needed to secure my final ladder, when Old Man Miller shuffled out of his condo downstairs - kitty-corner to mine. He ventured out of his unit a couple of times a day to take his cat for a walk on its leash. At first, seeing a cat on a leash was odd. Like, a slight against nature or something. Cats on leashes were contrary to all that being a cat was supposed to be, to my way of thinking. It seemed to me every time the cat's eyes met mine, it pleaded to be rescued and granted its freedom. But I liked Old Man Miller and he loved his cat, so I got used to it and never told him how wrong I thought it was.

"Morning, Mr. Miller," I shouted because he was hard of hearing and Ol' Bessie was loud.

"Well, top of the morning to you, missy. Off to work?" he asked.

"Sure am," I said, and jumped down from the running board. "I left you a bag of lemons and some fresh chamomile for tea by your planter."

I smiled as his eyes grew big, and he shuffled over to the white plastic bag full of goodies I'd left. I liked to bring little things so he knew someone was thinking about him. His family were jerks and never came around to visit. And since I knew how crappy that felt, I tried to do small niceties to help with the loneliness.

I slammed the door shut and walked toward the front of my mammoth vehicle when Mrs. Abernathy came around the corner with her little yapper. The cat and dog fought every time they saw each other. I didn't understand why she brought her little purebred to our side of the courtyard, because she lived in a completely different building. Unless she had alternative reasons that didn't include the pets.

"Great. Here comes trouble," Old Man Miller mumbled. I wanted to whisper back that I thought Mrs. Abernathy liked him, but he'd never hear me, and I sure wasn't shouting it at him with her standing only a few feet away.

On cue, her little precious began yapping, and Mr. Miller's cat hissed.

Instead, I yelled, "Some storm we had last night, eh?"

Old Man Miller looked at me. "Storm?"

"Don't tell me you managed to sleep through the lightning and thunder?"

"Must have, Cassandra. I'm thankful, too. Storms always make Bootsie here sketchy." He nodded to his black cat with white paws. "I'm surprised she didn't wake me up."

"Well, it was a real humdinger." I shivered.

Even though in the light of the day I'd moved past the nightmare, it still hung onto me. A sense of foreboding pressed heavily onto my chest.

My phone buzzed, and I looked to see who was texting me before my day had even begun.

"Sorry, can't make today. Will explain later." A text from my 'partner' Dawn. She was a very nice, very talented lady of leisure who only worked when she felt like it. She was married to a surgeon and didn't need to work, if she didn't want to. She was also the reason we had the job we were starting that morning.

This text meant I'd be arriving alone and that didn't make for a strong showing to the new client. A client, I might add, who had assigned me the nastiest staff member in his office to be my liaison. It was her job to make sure I got in and out with little hassle. But instead, she spent her time acting like I was causing her a huge inconvenience. It had been exceptionally hard dealing with her during the design process, and now that we were in the application phase, I couldn't imagine it would be any better.

I waved goodbye at the neighbors, who were too busy arguing with each other while their pets barked and hissed to notice me leaving. My SUV beater, who by now you know I affectionately referred to as Ol' Bessie, was ready to go.

Thankfully, it was a quick trip to the Capitol section of downtown Sacramento. As it was, my anxiety was through the roof.

That morning I was starting a job in the State Legislature's office. My work would be in the main conference room and seen by thousands of people in just a short amount of time. We had a strict deadline. I'd meticulously planned every single day and the timeline. To start the job on the very first day shorthanded ratcheted up my stress level.

I took a deep breath and held it for a few seconds, before exhaling slowly.

"Today will be fine. No, today will be magnificent. Everything will go better than I could ever imagine." I often talked myself down from whatever imaginary ledge I'd stumbled out onto. It helped to center me. As an afterthought, I added, "Even Stacy will be nice and helpful." That was the extent of my pep talk.

I arrived at the job and made my way through security. It took a bit to find the Legislature's staff member, Stacy, who had been assigned to me. Without giving me any hassle, she directed me to the back entrance and gave me the appropriate credentials so I could come and go with my supplies. Unfortunately, that took more than an hour to set up, so not only was I shorthanded, I was now running an hour behind.

Stacy left me to my own devices, and I was thankful for the sudden turnaround with her.

I worked my butt off getting my plaster hauled in, the ladders set up and my tools organized so I could jam through the rest of the morning until lunchtime. I'd decide then if I wanted to stop or skip lunch, eat a protein bar and keep going. I taped off my workspace and laid out plastic and tarps. I couldn't afford for anything to go wrong.

The first finish I was working on was in a bronze Italian limestone plaster, Marmorino. I needed to get this first layer on and then I could move to the ceiling. Looking around the room, I realized this room was going to take me all week to get just the lower portion done.

With my second deep sigh, I popped in my earbuds, cranked up my music, and said, "You can do this. You've got this. You know your stuff. Now, let's get this room done!"

And I went to work.

If I had any visitors that first part of the day, I wasn't aware of them. It wasn't unusual to have a few looky-loos peek in on me while I worked. People were fascinated with decorative painting and plasters. It didn't bother me, and if I had time, I'd even stop to answer their questions. So, either the staff member, Stacy, had kept everyone at bay, which I doubted, or I was so focused on my work, I didn't notice them.

I reached the end of the wall, and since my fingers were tingling again, I stepped back to make sure I had no thin spots for this first layer. I stretched my back and turned to wash my trowel and reload so I could start the next wall.

Wait.

I spun around the room and realized I'd actually managed to get the first layer down on all the walls, and it was probably the best base coat I'd ever applied. And I was good. I wasn't too modest to say I know my finishes and was an expert at applying them. So, when I say this was my best work, I mean it was good!

How in the heck did I get a week's worth of work done in one day?

I must have missed the building closing for the night. Surely it was after hours. I grabbed my phone and saw that it was just approaching noon. Lunchtime.

Lunchtime?

Was it still Monday? I spun around again in shock. I walked to the furthest wall and checked the corners to make sure they were even and tight.

Yep. No issues there. That was one hell of a pep talk I'd given myself!

I felt dizzy, a little tired, and the tips of my fingers were heading toward a painful tingle worse than they had when I'd awoken from the nightmare.

Maybe Dawn had shown up and done a couple of walls at super speed and then snuck out before saying anything. Maybe? There had to be a reasonable explanation.

I shook my head and decided that lunch was in order. Maybe I'd come back and this all would have been a dream. I'd have only completed one wall, and still have three more to go. I needed to eat and then check my blood sugar level anyway. I hadn't eaten breakfast after my morning shot and that was a no-no for me.

After finishing the cheese, almond butter celery sticks, and green bean salad I'd tossed into my cooler on the way out of the condo that morning, I grabbed my testing kit and insulin from my lunch cooler and headed to the restroom. I'd found over the years that testing my blood in public made people uncomfortable. Typically, I'd wait a couple of hours to test after eating, but since I'd not had breakfast and weird stuff was happening, I decided an early test wouldn't hurt. At least it would potentially rule out the possibility that I was in a diabetic coma and this was all a dream.

I'd been managing my blood levels all of my life. Being born with type one diabetes means I couldn't be squeamish or I'd die. People didn't understand how normal testing yourself and injecting life-saving insulin can become when it's a part of your life from the day you entered the world.

Keeping in the vein of the pep-talking I'd been giving myself, I said, "Come on, girl, your levels are going to be the best they've ever been. In fact, you're going to be so good, you'll not need your insulin today!" The tingling in my fingers had dimmed a bit after eating but now was back at it.

I shook my hands and smiled to myself because I always needed insulin. With my aching fingers crossed that the new slow-acting shot I'd taken that morning did its job, I went about testing my blood sugar levels. I must admit, I was a bit worried that all of the weird stuff going on was a result of the new meds my doctor had me on.

I drank some cold water. Closed my eyes and sat in silence for a moment. It was exactly what I needed.

I was now feeling clear-headed, my energy level was back to fantastic, and the tingling in my fingers had subsided. The latter was an indicator of poor circulation and that was never good. I had a sinking suspicion I was experiencing new side effects and that was the reason I was losing track of time, and forgetting things, like making my bed.

To my surprise, my blood level test came back great. Best ever, actually, even better than that morning, so I didn't need any additional insulin. Well, that was nice but discounted my theory about the side effects from my diabetes or the new meds.

I took care of business and got back to work. I was way ahead of schedule, so I decided to apply the base coat to the medallion and crown molding. I set about assembling my scaffolding. I'd erected it and taken it down hundreds of times on my own; it wasn't a problem for me to have it set up lickety-split.

Whatever the weird thing was that was happening to me, was working, so I popped my earbuds in and said, "Okay, girl, let's do this again. We're gonna base coat this entire room before the workday is done."

Even as I said the words, I didn't believe them. Nonetheless, I got busy.

And just like the first half of the day, I hummed and bopped around to the music playing in my ears and worked until I was done. I looked around the ceiling and walls, and sure enough, the base coat was on and perfectly too. Looking over my work for the day, I was mesmerized.

I glanced at my phone; it was fifteen minutes until quitting time. Just the perfect amount of workday left to clean my tools and pack up. I didn't know what kind of alternative universe today had become, but I decided to count my blessings and move forward.

After all, chances were this was all a dream, and I'd wake up any minute.

I washed up my tools and cleaned my workspace. I'd made arrangements to leave the room locked and my larger equipment there. Thankfully. It was a real pain to have to erect, disassemble, load, and unload my ladders and scaffolding, every single day. I'd done it many times - but this was so much easier.

Could this day get any better?

Chapter 6

Write your deepest wishes on seed infused paper and bury in your garden.

Water and tend to your dreams as they grown into fruition.

After the amazing day I had at my job, it was too much to

hope to beat the traffic home. Rush hour was the pits in the

state capitol, especially in this California summer heat.

I loaded up the tools and materials I didn't want to take a

chance might walk off with someone and hopped in my

vehicle. I rubbed the dashboard softly.

"Alright, Bessie, it's a real scorcher and bumper to bumper.

Sister, I need the air conditioner, so can you do me a real big

favor? Can ya get me home without anything going wrong

with you, please? I need you starting up tomorrow morning so

we can do this all over again."

I rubbed one more time for good measure and started her up.

Ol' Bessie had never let me down. She'd needed repairs and

plenty of maintenance but so far, she'd not left me stranded, ever.

At least not yet.

But even the optimist that I was, I knew eventually she was going to need a major repair. I took really good care of her, but she was an older girl, and cars broke down. Then I felt self-conscious, like I was jinxing myself for these negative thoughts, and rubbed her down once more and repeated my pep talk. I couldn't have this good luck day end on a bad note. In an attempt to control my thoughts, I buckled up, tuned up my driving home playlist, and got on the road.

Things were rolling along fairly slowly, with some gaps of twenty-five miles an hour, down to stop and go traffic. I disliked driving in traffic altogether but especially this sporadic stop and go. I couldn't find a rhythm, and I needed order in my life. Chaos was my nemesis. I'm sure it harkened back to the fact I was born with a pretty major health condition and had to live a fairly regulated existence to remain healthy. Order was necessary for my sanity. And my life.

Needless to say, I was pretty stressed out an hour into my drive. Things really took a turn for the worse when another driver swerved into my lane. Yeah, we were only going twenty miles an hour, but it was still a jerk move.

I slammed on my breaks and yelled, "Geez, dude! You need to stop!"

And he did. His car came to a sudden and immediate stop. Even though I'd already slammed on my brakes, I still managed to tap his bumper.

"Shoot," I yelled. "You've got to be kidding me! Bessie, I'm so sorry. You're okay, you're fine. You're a tough old broad. Nothing can be wrong with you, girl." I slipped from my SUV to see the damage.

"She's made of heavy metal. The other car is fiberglass," I muttered to myself. The car in front of me didn't move. As I approached, I could hear the motor as the driver gave it gas, but the vehicle wasn't going anywhere.

I arrived at the front of my car and the back of the other car whose motor was now revving alarmingly. Inspecting my front end, I saw that Ol' Bessie had suffered zero damage. Not even a small scratch. The relief was dizzying. I turned to check out the other car and noticed a small dent with a grey scrape. I looked back at where my bumper would have made the dent but saw nothing.

That was weird.

The driver folded out of his stranded car, and I noted how big he was. And, boy, was he pissed. Like, sweaty bald head, red ears, breathing hard kind of pissed.

I stepped back and said, "You stopped short in front of me."

"No shit, Sherlock!" the sweaty bald guy hollered. "It won't go. It's running, it's in gear, but it won't go." He slapped his hands on his head and spun around.

Every instinct in my body wanted away from him. So much so that I felt nauseated.

"Let's exchange information so we can get back on the road," I said. "It's too hot to stand out here."

He spun around and glared at me. "You think if I could get my car running, I'd be standing in the middle of the highway with *you*," he spat.

Well, one thing was for certain; I did not like him at all. I understood his frustration, but I didn't need his anger directed at me. If I knew anything, it was how not to be someone else's target.

He took a step towards me. "This is your fault!"

I shook my head and it began to pound. "No, you cut me off and stopped short in front of me."

"That's not my fault! I want my car to run. Are you so dim witted that you can't see that?"

He seemed to need to lay blame on someone and that someone was me. I didn't want anything to do with this. I was beginning to feel sick so I headed back to my vehicle. "Call someone."

I climbed in, locked my doors, and pulled away from him and his car, with my headache roaring in my ears. The pace was picking up a little, and I was able to merge into traffic and put a couple of exits between the jerk and myself.

Something was bugging me, but I didn't want to face it. This day had been weirder than any I'd had before, and I lived in California.

A giggle burst out of me.

I couldn't ever say aloud what I was thinking. I needed to eat a well-rounded meal, take a nice long shower and get a solid night's sleep so I could wake up in the morning and have things right back to normal.

Today would be a one-off.

You know, one of those unusual days, where most things went my way. What's so bad about that, anyway?

I decided to swing by the local farmer's market to pick up a few fresh veggies for dinner. I had a large package of scallops in the freezer to cook, along with whatever gems I discovered at the open-air market.

I found an excellent parking spot without having to ask out loud. Yay!

I parked and locked up Ol' Bessie. My tools were in her, and since I was not taking any chances, I placed my hand on my

SUV and said quietly, "You'll be fine here. Nothing will happen to you while I'm gone."

I looked around to make sure no one was watching and thought about my words, decided they were direct without being possibly harmful to others, and headed into the bustling rows of booths.

I skirted around and located the produce I was most interested in - asparagus, yellow and orange bell peppers, squash, and a small bag of fresh cherries. Being a diabetic, this was my version of candy. A girl needed her fruit too, and after the day I'd had, I deserved a treat.

After paying for my produce, I located a stand that offered a shot of lemongrass; it was delicious. Okay, fine, it wasn't delicious, but these were the games I played with myself because of my weird relationship with food. Namely, most American foods didn't like me. Or at least, my body didn't like them.

I headed back toward my SUV and walked past a margarita trailer that had several small tables set out to entice market-goers to stop and have a drink. My eye caught a booth next to it with colorful scarves and dried herbs hanging at various lengths around the perimeter.

The strong scents of lavender, silver sage, and frankincense were coming from the interior. The combination was seductive. My curiosity got the best of me, and I peeked behind one of the scarves. It was a feast for the senses. Giant crystals seemed to glow from each corner of the crowded booth. The ceiling held bundles of various dried herbs wrapped with different colored jute. The center table was filled with herbs for tea making, silver charms, and small crystals. Against the back wall a small table held an oversized book that looked like it had seen better days.

I started to walk toward the book when something glittered on the front table and drew me in. The smell of rosemary was strong where I found a lovely pink crystal on a rose gold chain. The crystal was wrapped in a soft gold wire with several black stones around the top where the chain fed through the eyelet. It was beautiful.

I'd seen many pieces similar to this before, but for some reason, this pink and gold piece drew me to it. I was reaching out to pick it up...

"Rose quartz is good for calming your mind and emotions," a quiet feminine voice came from a dark corner of the booth. She'd startled me, so I pulled my hand back.

I squinted in her direction and tried to make her out, but she was hidden behind several scarves, all I could construe was her shape. The woman appeared to be sitting with her back to the corner and had something wrapped around her.

Didn't she know how hot it was?

"I'm so sorry, I didn't see you there. It's a lovely piece. How much?" I asked.

The shadowed shape cocked her head and said, "One hundred and twenty gold pieces."

I withdrew my hand. First, I didn't have any gold. Second, one hundred and twenty dollars was way too much for this piece. You could find crystal pendants everywhere.

"Too much, eh?" the woman asked and cackled at me.

"I'm afraid that's out of my budget. It's beautiful, however. Did you make it?" I asked, and moved away from the pendant against my will. I made myself not look back. It was so hard; I wanted the dang thing.

"Yes, I made the piece. I made it for the one who pushes power into her words... and her alone."

That was cryptic. The hair on the back of my neck stood up. Did she just describe what I'd been avoiding all day?

I pretended to look around the booth at the other things the woman had available, but my gaze kept creeping back to the pendant. I could feel her eyes on me, and my fingertips began tingling. Up until now, tingling fingers didn't mean good things were in store for me. I settled on some delicious-smelling chamomile tea so I could get out of there and away from her. My luck had run out; as I was paying, the old woman started on the hard sell.

"You'll need the hematite along with the rose quartz to center yourself and deal with the shocks to come. Take care of your emotions. They are your friend and your enemy."

The hair on my arms stood up.

I handed over the money for the tea and said, "I appreciate your words of wisdom." I gave her a fake smile and tried to see her through the shadow she remained cloaked in.

She passed my bag of tea over. I noticed her hands looked young, and her nails were a perfect French manicure that didn't seem to match the voice.

I took the bag of tea she held out for me, and she grabbed my wrist, hissing, "Your words have power. Focus your emotions, Witch."

I pulled my hand away from the woman who was, at this point, freaking me out.

"I'm not a witch," I said.

"Do no harm," she hissed at me.

"Thank you for the tea." I grabbed the bag from her quickly and left her booth.

I wasn't a witch. I mean, I didn't have any problem with whatever religion, lifestyle, or faith people wanted to practice, but that didn't change the fact that I wasn't a witch.

I decided I'd had enough of the market and headed to my car. The hair on the back of my neck was standing up, and I was rattled. I slid my sunglasses on my nose and looked around. No one stood out to me, but the uneasiness continued. I walked quickly to my car and got in as fast as I could. I wasn't able to relax until I was safely locked inside with Ol' Bessie's motor purring.

I looked at the bags in the passenger seat that held my dinner and decided I needed to get home and test my blood sugar level. I'd had such an easy day; I'd not been as diligent as I should have been. I was probably reading too much into the weird happenings.

I picked up the tea and noticed it felt too heavy for a bag of dried chamomile tea. I tried to open the sealed bag so I could peer inside, but no matter what angle I came at it, the bag refused to open.

I hated it when the simplest of tasks became so complicated. Since I was already talking to inanimate objects to make things work the way I wanted, I took a deep breath and said, "Open."

And it did.

The bag I'd been struggling with popped open allowing me to see the rose quartz crystal and rose gold chain nestled at the bottom.

"She made a mistake. She must have." This felt weird. I knew beyond all doubt the woman had done this on purpose, and I wasn't having it.

On a deep sigh, I stuffed my other bags behind the passenger seat, out of view, and set off to the booth where the tea lady was located. I passed the veggie vendor I'd bought my produce from, the lemongrass stand, and the margarita booth with tables. I smiled at the long line. A frozen frosty drink would be good right about now, but the alcohol and sugar would be way too much for me.

I reached the space that should have been the tea lady who'd called me a witch and found a blanket vendor.

First, who the heck sold fluffy hot blankets during a California summer?

Second, where was the tea lady?

"I must have buzzed by her while musing over the margarita," I said to myself.

I retraced my steps and every time ended back up at the blanket booth.

Were there two margarita vendors? Two margarita vendors next to identical lemongrass stalls?

I looked back and forth, up and down the row, and didn't know what to do. I had a necklace that didn't belong to me, and now its owner had vanished into thin air.

I looked back down at the bag in my hand and sighed. "I guess you're mine now. You must have been meant for me, right? That's the way it works, isn't it?"

I knew speaking to the pendant wouldn't bring the lady back, but it did make me feel marginally better about taking something that wasn't mine to take.

I wondered as I put Bessie into gear, what the chances were that I could make it home without any other strange occurrences.

Chapter 7

Cleanse your crystals and alter stones in salt water under a full moon, for

clarity and energy.

The pendant haunted me. Tortured me, really. The thing was
driving me insane.

I'd come home after the farmer's market without thinking
much more about it. I'd set about making dinner, and when I
took my plate of scallops and roasted vegetables to the small
table on my postage-stamp sized deck, there it was, sitting on
the table, refracting the last beams of sunlight.

I hadn't brought it outside. And I was becoming more
confident the weird stuff that was happening ...was really
happening. I wasn't dreaming. I wasn't having a diabetic
episode, nor were these hallucinations from the new meds.
These cool but weird things were truly happening to me. I'd
somehow gained the ability to speak over events I wanted to
influence. The knowledge was heady, to say the least, so in
order to keep myself in check, I'd made a decision to enjoy

the power my words seemed to wield, and ignore the rest as long as I could.

What else was I supposed to do? I couldn't go to the police. What would I tell them? I couldn't go to my doctor and ask to have my head examined. What proof did I have that my words were making things happen? I didn't think a seventy-two-hour hold in the psych ward was going to help anyway.

Over the next few days, that damned necklace began appearing everywhere I went. I knew it was part of all the crazy that was swirling around me.

The thing was pretty and all, but it was scaring me. It showed up in my car, toolbox, lunch box, and finally, after my long day, I found it laying on the nightstand next to my bed.

I decided using my newfound gift was in order. After putting it away several times and it reappearing on its own accord, it was time to push my will. I looked it dead in the crystal and said, "Stay in the drawer." Then I placed it in its original bag, put that in a small box, which I placed in the bottom drawer of my dresser.

I felt chances were pretty good it would stay. Since discovering my new power with words, nothing had gone against me.

The woman who'd given me the pendant had said, "Do no harm." Those words played over and over in my mind. I thought they were important. I thought back to my conversation with her and wished I'd not reacted emotionally, but had spent time talking with her and asking questions. She seemed to know what was happening, at least more than I did.

So here I was, three days after the woman had slipped me the pendant, and I was losing my mind.

I couldn't stop thinking about it. I went to the drawer four separate times to pull it out before I realized what I was doing. I dreamed about it. I found myself thinking about it in the shower, during conversations, while driving. It was all I could do not to rip it out of the drawer and wear it. Just the thought of doing that brought relief. Twice, I was out running errands and found myself heading home to get the crystal.

I felt I'd entered a new reality. Like, it was the same planet I'd always lived on, with the same things and people... but different. Now there had been this entire new system introduced, and I was connected to it somehow. And I couldn't blame the necklace. It had already started before I'd received it. In fact, one could argue the necklace came because of this new thing I was involved in. And obviously, I wasn't alone. I knew others were involved, too, because of the necklace giver.

As my obsession with the necklace grew, I decided I needed to find someone to help me with it. I had a bunch of questions that needed answers. How did one go about finding a mystical person? Was a fortune teller still a thing? Once upon a time, I'd see their tiny storefronts all over, but these days, they seemed to be a thing of the past. I decided it was worth a chance to at least look for one and see how I felt. I mean, what could it hurt, anyway?

I found three who fit the bill by searching online. Two were in Sacramento, but one was located in the town over from mine, just south of Sacramento in Elk Grove. I called the number on the website, and no one answered. There was no voicemail set up. I couldn't leave her a message, so I decided to drive by on my way home from work.

The job was going really well. It was light years ahead of schedule. Every morning I arrived at work and made a statement that was reasonable but would propel me forward. It was working, and I was learning to use my words sparingly. I was sure the universe would apply some kind of balance, or tax, for whatever I made happen, and I didn't know what that would look like. I did know I needed to be careful.

I arrived at the small storefront as the sun was setting and an hour before its sign said it closed. It was still warm out, but chills ran over every inch of my body as I stepped through the doorway. The interior was very similar to the booth where I'd mistakenly received the pendant. A round table sat at the center of the room with a counter against the back wall. A set of floor-length curtains blocked what I thought looked to be a doorway to another room.

Multi-colored scarves hung from the windows, blocking out any hope sunlight might have had of making its way into the room. More colorful scarves covered every surface. The ceiling had various dried herbs hanging, and the scent was exactly the same as the booth's had been. Crystals in numerous shapes and sizes sat atop the scarves on the center table, along with a single deck of tarot cards.

There wasn't anyone in the main room, and I didn't feel comfortable snooping around in the back, so I said, "Hello." Honestly, I should have known right then this was a bust. Wouldn't a fortune teller know when someone came into her shop?

"Welcome," a deep voice said from the curtained doorway. There stood one of the best-looking men I'd ever seen, wiping his mouth. He was tall, pale, well built with broad shoulders and short-styled blond hair, crystal blue eyes, and he wore a well-fitted black suit with a white shirt unbuttoned to his chest.

Yes, he was that good-looking, and I took it all in.

"Hi, are you the fortune teller?" I asked once I got over my shock.

"I am," he replied. He pulled a chair out from the round table, sat down, and began shuffling the deck without taking his eyes off of me. "My name is Rolfe. Can I read your cards?"

"Well, actually, I was hoping you could help me. Or, point me in the direction of someone who could help me."

"There is a price for everything." He set the deck down and folded his arms.

"Oh, of course. I'm happy to pay for any information you can give me."

He studied me for a moment. "How can I help?"

I sat in the chair across from him and removed the pendant to show him. As with anytime my skin came in contact with the cold metal, a jolt traveled from my fingers to my heart. I swear it skipped a beat. I laid the pendant on the table.

"A very mysterious woman gave this to me. Well, truth be told, I didn't want it, so she slipped it into my bag." My eyes were riveted to the pendant. I fought the urge to snatch it back and put it around my neck.

He didn't move to pick it up, but his eyes were glued to it as well. "Who did you say gave this to you?"

I shrugged. "Some lady at the open-air market in Sac. When I went back to return it, she was gone. Or I couldn't find her booth, anyway."

"How long have you had it in your possession?" He still hadn't made a move to pick it up.

I broke out in a sweat. I wanted him to look at me, not the pendant. My palms began to itch, and my leg bounced from the energy my nerves had pulsing through my body. I felt my heartbeat in my throat. I reached out and snatched the pendant off the table and shoved it in my pocket.

Rolfe looked at me for the first time since showing him the pendant. He shook his head and whispered, "It had me in its thrall."

"It can hear you. Even if we whisper," I whispered back.

Rolfe cocked his head. "Tell me exactly where you got it again."

I spent the next several minutes recounting how I'd obtained the piece of jewelry. I told him everything about how I wanted it, eventually got it, and even quipped about stroking it and calling it "my precious." I joked about it, but it wasn't too far from the truth. I can't explain why, but I left out what the woman said to me about it. I didn't tell him that she called me a witch or that she said it was for me. I also didn't tell him about my newfound influence.

"The first thing I'd tell you to do is to cleanse it in saltwater. It will help negate any bad energy that might be surrounding the piece. Also, set your own intention for it while you wash it. A day in the sunlight wouldn't hurt it either. One thing's for sure. Its charm isn't just focused on you. I couldn't take my eyes off of it. A part of me wants to force you to give it to me even now that it's hidden from view."

I stood abruptly. The need to flee was overwhelming. I couldn't fight it *and* the desire to wear the pendent. I turned on my heel and ran the few steps to the door.

"Wait!" I heard as I slammed the door closed behind me.

I braced my hands on my knees and worked hard to stabilize my breathing. I glanced behind me at the door; it was going to open any minute. He would try to take it from me. I couldn't have anyone coming for my pendant.

"Stay inside." Pictures of a man starving to death inside his own shop flooded my brain along with the words, "Do no harm."

"Stay inside until I'm gone," I whispered, hoping that would counter the first instruction. Dammit. Now I was going to have to check on him later.

I decided the thing to do was what I should have done in the first place and consult the internet. Surely someone online would have some idea what I was supposed to do next.

A website, blog, or Facebook group. Something besides letting anyone else lay their eyes on my crystal. I just couldn't have it. It wasn't until I was home and deep down a black hole of witchcraft and magic that didn't help me in the slightest, other than to confirm cleansing it in salt water would help, I remembered something. I'd never paid Rolfe the fortune teller. While he didn't actually offer me anything to go on, he might still.

Guess I really was going back.

Chapter 8

Charge your crystals in the full sun for several hours to capture their full

power.

The hairless creature scraped his knees across the blood-

soaked stone. Screams of pain and despair filled the heavy air

around him. Dirt-caked hands reached through the bars

attempting to grab him as he dragged his body by the cages.

He was careful to stay in the middle. If they laid their hands

on him, Master Zeifrus would be outraged.

He couldn't suffer his Master's wrath. He might not survive

such an assault again.

He reached the large flat stone where his Master was working

and used the jagged troll bone protruding from the cave wall

to pull himself up. Master didn't like to be inconvenienced by

having to look down at his servant.

"The Oracle desires your presence, Master."

"What could possibly be more important than my work here?" the Master roared and slapped a bloody hand down on the corpse flayed out before him on the stone slab.

"Master, the Oracle has scried a possible candidate."

"You're sure?" the Master asked.

The creature cringed at the question. Truth was, he wasn't sure. He was only a messenger. He had no idea if the Oracle could be trusted. Those decisions were so far above him, he'd not even stopped to think about it until this very moment.

"The... the... the Oracle said it could be one of the Thirteen." The creature bowed as low as he could without letting go of the cave wall.

Master Ziefrus threw his crude stone knife down on the body and whipped around to leer directly at the cowering servant who'd interrupted him.

"The Oracle will be right, or you'll find yourself in one of those cages awaiting your turn on the slab."

The trembling creature prostrated itself lower and fell to the wet floor. Master Ziefrus snarled at it as it dragged itself into the shadows and out of view. Turning on his heel, the sound of his large boots splashing through the thick blood-covered floor bounced around the large cavern as he headed toward the skull and bone-lined corridor.

"Sigt!" he bellowed. He grabbed a fire torch from its sconce to light his way as he stomped through the thick slime of decay that gathered at the entrance of the tunnel.

"Master Ziefrus," the low rumble bounced off the skeletal walls.

"The Oracle may have scried one of the Thirteen. You must reach her before the Witch does. Bring her to me for the incantation. I need her alive."

"Does she have use of her magic?"

"Unknown as of yet."

"Unharmed?" Sigt's disembodied voice inquired.

"Alive. I care not what you do to her as long as she arrives to me breathing. I'll send coordinates once I have them."

"As you wish, Master."

"Sigt," Master Ziefrus said. "On second thought, I want you to play with her. Broken is how I desire her when she arrives at her final destination. Broken but breathing"

"As you command, so it shall be."

Master Ziefrus rounded a corner and descended the narrow stone staircase most of his creatures and creations wouldn't dare venture down. The ceiling of the stairway carved into the cave was slick with dripping bodies. The sound of his heavy boot falls reverberated, sending smaller creatures scurrying. Best they do not capture the attention of this Master.

The winding staircase opened up into a large cavern. Bodies of multiple creatures hung from the ceiling in varying stages of rot.

He took a deep breath. He loved the smell of decay. Its sweet, pungent aroma was thick in the closed quarters.

A heavy chain moved in the furthest recesses of the cavern.

"What news called me away from my work?" Master Ziefrus asked.

The thick metal scraped the stone floor as a hunched creature moved its bulbous body from the shadows.

"I scried this day, as I have all the days since my capture, Master"

"And?"

"A candidate has emerged. A human. The location is on the stand." He pointed a thin long talon to a small flat stone table, where a lone sheet of parchment lay.

"Human?" Master Ziefrus barked, retrieving the coordinates. "How is that possible?"

"I know not, Master. Only that this creature lives among humans and carries the markers."

"Is it possible she is the result of a Natural mating with a human?"

"Possibly," the creature said, and began shuffling back into the shadows of its cave, the chain slowing his progress.

"Is she the first of the Thirteen?"

"Possibly," the Oracle's voice trailed off.

"When will we know?"

Master Ziefrus strained to hear the oracle's reply.

"When you bring her to me."

Ziefrus examined the display of wings strung around the cavern. Fae, fairy, sprites, and even a solitary set of the priceless dragon flyers. It was not the first time he mused at the oracle's obsession with wings since Ziefrus had cut his own from his body. It pleased him to know the creature suffered after all these centuries shackled in the cave. He glanced back at the dragon flyers. They'd come in handy when he needed to trade for a spell. Dark magic makers loved extinct items. Yes, these would come in very handy.

They were close. He could feel it. One of the Thirteen broadcasting her location had to be a direct result of the first strike against the Witch.

Could be the attack had had an unknown effect. Would another attack bring the candidate closer to the surface? This was the closest they'd ever been to locating one of the Thirteen.

His intuition was yelling at him to move quickly. He always listened to his intuition.

"Sigt!" Ziefrus shouted, and retraced his path up the slime-covered stone steps. "I have the coordinates!"

Chapter 9

Fill a clear jar with clean water and set it out under a full moon, add charged crystals for extra power. Drink a glass to start your day.

"**W**e must send wolves after her right away." Elsie finished writing, closed her Book of Shadow, and turned away from the dark wood podium to face Max.

"Potential guardians."

"Has she come into her magic?" he asked as he wandered around the room, studying the scrying maps hanging on the dark wood walls on either side of the vast shelves of grimoires the Witch had collected over the centuries. Powerful magic was held in this room.

The newer maps were birchwood, while some of the more ancient maps were burned onto hides. The ceiling tapered off into a point high above. The opposite wall from the entrance featured six tall thin arched windows that jutted out to create a space where a smaller table filled the area. The wall that hosted the doorway was covered with shelves of old leather-bound grimoires. Ornately carved dark wood-lined the walls where the maps hung. The same dark carved wood made up the vast bookshelves and framed the thick leaded glass windows.

Bane jars sat in each corner of the room and served as extra protection. Max shivered. He'd go up against any creature in the world happily, but he'd never try to break into or attack a witch in her own home. Not only would it be deadly, but it would also be a long, painful death. One he never wanted to experience.

"She must, to some degree, at least. She lit up like a neon light the moment I scried. Her exact location became apparent immediately, and that means anyone can find her. If we don't reach her first, they will kill her."

"That can't happen." Max braced his hands on the scrying table and studied the map.

Elsie joined Maximillian at the round table centered in the large room. On it lay a drawing of modern California burned into an oversized parchment made of Birchwood. Its bark ends curled over the edge of the table. She chose a large raw diamond that caught the sunlight streaming in from the high thick windows. It was attached to a heavily ornate silver chain that unfolded as she held it over the birchwood map.

"No, it cannot. We need to send wolves who know how to handle themselves and are willing to receive a protection mark from me."

"That won't be a problem."

"I think you should go too."

"I'm not leaving you."

"We've been separated for centuries. I can protect myself. The awakening of the Thirteen must be our focus."

"You are under attack as well, and just as important as they are. If not more. I shan't leave you again. Matters not what words of persuasion you attempt to use against me." He stepped forward and took her free hand. "Now that I have you back, I'm never leaving your side."

"Maximillian, I see now that sending you away was harmful to us. But we must do what we promised when we initiated the death slumber spell."

"When we all agreed to this, it was because humans had destroyed all but one of the covens. Thousands of witches were wiped off the face of the earth because of cruel hysteria. If we'd made the decision to hide or keep fighting, you might not be standing here today. And if that were the case, none of us would have survived."

Elsie took in her wolf's broad shoulders and knew he carried the weight of their survival on them.

"I understand. But I don't know the other wolves. I only know you. I know you'll fight to the death to keep her alive. I need you to do that for her."

Max placed her hand against his chest and stepped closer. "I only fight to the death for you, Elsie. No one else."

"Maximillian..." He was the only one she trusted. Elsie never doubted Max and his strength. He'd never disappointed her...even after centuries of her disappointing him. She stepped closer yet to her Wolf and laid her head against his chest in order to hear his heart. The only heart that had ever been synced to her's. Hearing its sure and steady staccato calmed her.

"I won't be swayed on this. But, I will send Alicaster Blue, along with one older wolf and one younger."

"Only three? It's not enough."

"It will have to be."

"Send five, at least."

"I'll send four. Alicaster Blue, Thaddeus; an older wolf, and two younger; Anton and Roan; one is the best tracker I have, and the other is the best fighter of the younger wolves. Will that suffice?"

She dropped her head. "It'll have to, I suppose."

"Do you trust me?"

"Of course, I do."

"Then hear my pledge to bring this first one home to you."

She looked at him. "I'd be more comforted if it were you leading the charge."

Elsie centered the scrying stone over the map and chanted, "*Shu metti lolia.*"

The stone whipped out of her hand and fell heavily onto the map.

She looked at her wolf. "See. There is no question where she is."

"Why now?" He furrowed his brow as he examined where the diamond landed. "Have you performed the awakening spell?"

"No, I was waiting for the wolves to settle into position beforehand. Max, if I can see her...so can anyone with scrying abilities."

"Time is of the essence." Max placed his hands on the table and leaned closer, his handsome features serious and concentrated on the diamond.

"I'm afraid we may already be too late." The faint hint of hopelessness in Elsie's voice spurned Max into action.

"Luckily, she isn't far," he gently reassured her. "I'll organize the wolves."

"I'll grab my bones. I have a fresh batch of *maginka* waiting to be used."

"You mean, after all this time, you haven't upgraded to needles?"

"No, why would I use anything but my bones?"

Max shrugged. "Modernization?"

Elsie rolled her eyes and pointed to the map. "I just used a seven-hundred-year-old uncut Egyptian diamond to scry the location of a burgeoning witch on a magical birch wood map and you're questioning my *marking* tools?"

"Tattoos."

"What?"

"They're called tattoos now."

Elsie's glowing eyes turned to Maximillian. "My *marking* will guard your wolves against magical foes, and allow you to transform into multiple creatures... They are not *tattoos.*"

"The rest of the world thinks they're tattoos," Max said with a smirk.

"The rest of the world is mistaken." She narrowed her eyes. "It's time you get into the modern age, Witch."

"My manner of doing things might be old-fashioned but they are effective. I think I'll hang onto my ways if you please," she said.

Max smiled, he enjoyed poking fun at her. She was stunning when she was mad. He liked her stunning. And when she was mad, she wasn't worrying, and since this was their last stand, he'd enjoy every second of it. He felt it in the deepest recesses of his soul. Whatever the outcome, when this war was done... well, it was his last. If Elsie no longer walked this earth, neither would he. She foresaw her future, and, in turn, his too. He'd never let her sever their bond. He'd die first.

"Study the area and alert your wolves. We can't afford to waste any more time."

Elsie left the scrying chamber and passed the large kitchen where a few of the younger wolves were preparing their morning meal. The scent of males in her home felt right. Witches lived in covens and wolves in packs. Neither species was meant to live a solitary life. But she had. And she'd suffered.

At least she'd had the creatures she saved to keep her company. And work.

"My work is too important to worry about feelings of loneliness," she admonished herself out loud. "Too much to do. Too many lives to save."

"Ma'am," one of the wolves said. She would need to remember about canine hearing. She'd lived too long alone and muttering to oneself became a habit.

"Who might you be?"

"My name is Roan, ma'am."

The young wolf was huge by a mortal man's standard. Dark brown hair, bright green eyes, and a full sensuous mouth made for a striking face. Thankfully, he wore a short dark beard or he'd be almost too pretty to take seriously.

"I believe you're one of the wolves going after our first awakening. I'm heading to fetch my *marking* bones now. Would you mind assisting me?"

Before he could answer, several other broad shoulders crammed into the doorway.

"You'll be *marking*, then?" one of the wolves who'd shoved his way to the front asked.

"Will you be giving shifter *markings*?" another shouted from behind the crowd.

Elsie smiled. "I'm afraid this time they will be runes of protection, and only for those going on the quest."

"Are you taking volunteers?"

"I'll go!"

"What can I do to get a bird *mark*?"

"I'd do anything for an eagle's *mark*!"

The wolves were talking at once, and she was unable to answer before another asked a question.

"That's enough," growled Max from behind Elsie. "Roan, go grab Thaddeus and Alicaster Blue and join us in the witch's *marking chamber*."

The young wolf made a move to do as requested and turned back. "Where is the *marking* chamber?"

"It's the stone building near the edge of the blackberry patch," Elsie turned to Max. "The chamber is cleansed and ready. I only need help moving my bones and *maginka* back into the chamber. I can set it up."

"I'll help."

"Me too."

"Can I watch you *mark* him?"

"Anton, help Elsie move her equipment and set up. You'll be first," Max instructed. The young wolf howled, and Max smiled to himself.

"They've been bored stiff. Don't begrudge them what little fun they might have before the danger arrives," Max whispered to Elsie.

A tall wolf pushed his way to stand in front of Elsie. He was also dark-haired, but his hair was past his shoulders. He had dark brown eyes, clear skin that featured a square jaw, high cheekbones, and a bright white smile. She'd forgotten how attractive wolves were by nature. Her awakening witches didn't stand a chance.

"Please follow me. Any who wish to watch may do so, but only in silence. I must be able to concentrate so I don't *mark* him with a rune that does nothing more than to protect him from a mouse."

She smiled and led the way. The wolves howled with laughter and followed behind. As in, all of them. She realized this when she stopped halfway up the winding staircase and was almost knocked over.

"Anton is helping me - the rest of you can meet us at the *marking* chamber. It's the stone building out by the blackberry patch." She repeated Max's earlier instruction. The wolves turned and ran back down the staircase at supernatural speed.

"Will I be getting a shifter *mark* too?" Anton asked.

"I'm afraid those *marks* are only given by a bonded witch to her guardian."

"But you're the only witch. Can many of us bond with you so we can receive the *mark*?"

"In the past, it wasn't unusual for a Witch to bond with several Wolves throughout her life, and yes, she could offer her guardians any *marking* she chooses. But now, we have young witches coming, and I'd never want to bond with one of you if one of them could. As it is, our new witches will probably need to bond with several of you just to stay alive."

"Can't you bond with us and then let the new witches bond with us too?"

A reasonable question, she thought.

"I'm afraid it isn't that simple. The bonding ceremony is intense and takes a lot of magic. The *markings* that come from the bonds are unique to the witch and her guardians. Think of it as being very intimate."

"Is it like a marriage?"

"Not like a human marriage. The bonded pair may be physically intimate with one another, but they don't have to." She thought for a moment and nodded her head. "Almost half I'd say did, to be truthful. But it's not a requirement."

They reached the top of the stairs. She led them to the room where her equipment was stored and opened the heavy door. "There are many gifts a witch gives her guardian for keeping her safe. The biggest gift, of course, is the ability for a wolf to shift into other beings. But you must understand every witch has her own style and magic. I can't do anything that might interfere with one of the awakening witch's desire to choose a guardian."

"I just want to fly. To soar high above the trees, like Max does. It's something I've always wanted," Anton said.

She turned to the young wolf and placed her hand against his chest. "Remember, when the girls wake up from their death slumber, they won't know anything. They will be depending on you all to guide them safely here."

"We won't let you down. I swear it."

She put her head down. For sure some of them would. She knew they weren't all coming out of this alive.

"Here we go. Can you take these two boxes and I'll grab the bags?" She pointed to two large wooden boxes with lids that would be much too heavy for a mortal man, but that a wolf could handle with no problem.

The wolf took the boxes, and she took the bags, and they headed out to the *marking* chamber.

As she watched the young eager wolf bound down the stairs carrying her marking bones, she began to realize how unprepared they were for the coming war.

When they reached the stone building, most of the wolves were gathered and waiting. The *marking* chamber had a slate roof and floors, slate walls, and ceiling. The floor sloped slightly to the center where a drain had been installed. It was the perfect room for experimenting on new spells. Easy clean-up.

Several of them rushed forward to relieve her of her bags. Realizing from that point on she'd have an audience, she went about setting up her chamber and allowed the wolves to help when they could. She couldn't blame them. This was all part of their history too. The history they'd lost because she'd refused Max.

"Anton, have a seat." She rolled out the dragon hide that had held her bones for near millennia and, with power in her voice, said, *"Sentia liviniste."*

The bones were so old, they weren't even ivory anymore. The stain of time and magic had left the razor-sharp tools various shades of deep blue. Pride swelled in her chest. She had the most impressive marking collection. One that only an ancient witch could amass.

She chose one of the smaller needles from the hide and moved to where the *maginka* was located on a small counter with a built-in slate sink.

"What are you sitting on?" Max roared. He stepped into the small chamber with Roan, Alicaster Blue who she recognized, and one other wolf she assumed must be Thaddeus.

Anton jumped from his seat and bounced between his feet. "What's wrong with the seat? I upgraded. I thought you'd be pleased," the Last Witch said, looking down at her freshly painted wooden chair she'd purchased from a local furniture maker.

"I had to sit on a single peg stool for every single one of my marks, and they get this throne?"

She rolled her eyes. "It's hardly a throne. Sit," she said to Anton.

"Where's the stool?" Max growled and stepped forward.

Anton's head swiveled back and forth as he watched the two, unable to decide which way was going to net him the least amount of trouble.

"Are you serious?" Elsie asked.

"I sat on that uncomfortable monstrosity for every single one of my markings. You made me. Every time I complained about it, you told me to wolf up. I think you even referred to me as a cub once. If I had to endure that for my *markings*, the least they can do is the same."

The group of wolves howled in unison, except Maximillian. He watched Elsie with a predatory stare.

"I'll not retrieve it, and I'll not tell you where it is, either," she said above the howling.

"So, you still have it."

"Of course, I do."

"It should be here."

"It's my property, and I'll say when it's used and when it's not. Right now, it's not!" The howling stopped. Elsie lowered her glowing silver eyes, and her voice quivered with power. She pointed to Anton. "Sit." He promptly obeyed.

"I'll allow you to stay if you behave yourselves." She turned her eyes around the room, allowing them all to get a good look at her. "Any more howling, and you'll go."

Max growled at Anton, "Stand up." The younger wolf sprung to his feet. Max grabbed the chair and stormed out of the door.

Anton looked to Elsie and shrugged his shoulders.

Max returned carrying a log and set it on end in the middle of the room.

"Balance on that," he growled at Anton. "Be a wolf."

Max snarled at Elsie. She rolled her eyes and attached the bone to the glass *maginka* container.

She gently placed her hand on Anton's shoulder. Max growled again.

"Brace yourself," she whispered.

Chapter 10

Boil slices of lemon and citronella to cleanse the air in your home.

Max stood over each of the four wolves as they received their first *marking* from the Last Witch. He growled the entire time. Seemed the old wolf didn't like his witch *marking* anyone else but him. Sure, he knew it was for the greater good, but the wolf in him couldn't stand her being that close and touching anyone but himself. He'd been without her for far too long. The realization he'd have to endure this on a regular basis drove him to make a promise to himself to get all of the Thirteen home and linked up with their own guardians so he didn't have to go through this again. He'd managed to keep her alive through all the wars they had fought together without any other help. Now there was a great possibility she'd take on another guardian and that wouldn't stand for him.

Being a Wolf was hard.

He looked around at the crowd and back at Elsie, who was finishing up with Alicaster Blue. Her low chanting was mesmerizing. As soon as she'd begun, the room had gone quiet. The three who'd already received their rune marks of protection were outside the marking chamber vomiting. They'd be sick for a few hours.

This was one of the most rewarding experiences a guardian would ever know, but also the most painful. The younger wolves only saw how freeing it was to be able to take flight, or shift into a bear, a horse, or lion; they hadn't yet seen all that the wolf who receives the marks went through - the pain, the pressure, the commitment.

She chose to place the rune on the lower hip and made it as small as possible without compromising its protection.

"*Shuntee mila molki lanni blees,*" the Last Witch chanted, enchanting the onlookers.

Her razor-sharp bones dove deep into the flesh she was currently working on. Each mark penetrated well past layers of skin and deep into the muscle to deliver the *maginka*. It was the only way to ensure the magic was forever. The spell would become part of the wolf's DNA. A piece of his being. Every mark changed him just a little. Until finally, if he was lucky enough to live a long life as a guardian, he'd be covered with markings and changed forever.

As was Max. Changed forever by the Witch, he'd pledged his life to protect.

He watched her gift her magic to another. Truth be told, he'd never seen her mark anyone else, him being the only guardian she'd ever taken. They'd been the most resourceful and adaptable of their kind... now they were the most powerful. Chosen to stay behind and bring the Thirteen forward when it was time.

Those three centuries had passed slowly.

She'd sent him away so easily. Forced them both to go much too long without each other. It was unnatural. But then again, they had been trying to survive the massacre they'd suffered at the hands of the humans. Max shook his head and brought his focus back to the room. He needed to move forward from the past and leave it there. It wasn't going to help his pack, or the Witches, if he didn't stay connected to the here and now.

Alicaster Blue was covered in sweat and gritting his teeth. His hands clenched hard, knuckles white. His heavy boot bounced in an effort to release energy.

"Have you been *marked*, Blue?" Max asked.

"Only once," he ground out. "A protection rune against Vampire."

"Who could have known how valuable that would end up being?" Max barked.

"My Witch knew." He looked to his Alpha and growled.

"Saved my life, time and again."

"Hopefully this rune will be just as effective," Elsie said, setting her marking bones on the counter. "How do you feel? You seem to be doing much better than your pack mates."

She opened a cupboard and removed a clean ivory towel and a vial. She used the towel to wipe away the blood from the intricate rune she'd placed on his body and sprinkled the contents of the vial over the new mark.

"*Hep lemme sikin.*" She blew softly against the mark. A clear coating covered the rune and immediately softened the pain.

"Thank you!" Alicaster Blue ran his eyes over the Witch.

"Why'd you let the others suffer?"

"They need to have a crash course in what receiving a witch's magic feels like. If they believe they want so many markings that will give them the ability to transform, then they need to understand what they are in store for."

She handed him a small crystal. "You've done your time and suffered more anguish than most alive today. Your loss is our loss, Blue."

"You knew my witch, Samantha of Havenshire?"

"I knew of her. She was older than me. But I remember her being a brave warrior. She saved thousands of human lives during the Blood Wars."

"Indeed, she did." Alicaster Blue stood tall and took the Last Witch's hand, ignoring Max's warning growl. "I pledge my life to the Thirteen. I *will* find them and bring them together, alive."

Elsie placed her hand on the large wolf's chest. "I know you will, Blue. I have foreseen it," she whispered, her face turned up to his.

He looked at the crystal she'd placed in his hand. It was clear on one end and faded to a deep blue on the other. It was warm. He could feel its power pulsating as if it was a living being.

She folded both of her small hands around his large hand that held the crystal and said, *"Sterum tractum le meta."* The crystal grew hot and then at once was ice cold. The Last Witch looked up into his face and whispered, "You honor us with your devotion."

"Ah!" Alicaster Blue snarled as the crystal seared through his palm to embed itself inside his hand.

She let go and stepped back. "Now I'll be able to track you all as long as you stay together. Even during a shift."

Elsie turned away from Alicaster Blue and addressed Max, "I need the four in here, and everyone else out."

"You heard her. Everyone out." Max shuffled out of the building, along with the groaning wolves who were upset they had to leave and found the three cleaning themselves. "She's ready for you."

Once they had assembled inside, Max closed the door.

"When you find her, she isn't going to believe you. She is a modern woman, believing she is human. It wouldn't normally be safe for a woman to venture off with four rather large men, regardless of your natural appeal." She looked around the group and caught each one of the wolves in his eye. "It's imperative you don't frighten her."

"Can't we just take her? I mean, right now, she's just a human female. Should be a pretty easy grab and go, if you know what I mean," Anton asked on a laugh, and looked around for agreement.

Elsie hissed, *"Stemi zini moross!"*

Eyes glowing silver she thrust her hands out palm forward in Anton's direction. He flew backward against the stone wall, sending bottles and vials filled with potions, assorted bits of dried bugs, and herbs crashing to the floor.

"Watch your mouth," the Last Witch said in a voice that welcomed no opposition or discussion. "If time wasn't of the essence, I'd mark another wolf and pull you from this quest."

Maximillian growled at his young pack member and stalked toward him. Anton relaxed back against the wall that was half holding him up and waited for the punishment that would come. One of these days, his mouth was going to get him killed. Why he had to say everything that came into his head, he didn't know. By now you'd think he'd know better.

Max grabbed him by the shirt and threw him toward the middle of the room. "Not another word from you or I'll expel you myself."

The Last Witch removed a large crystal, a leather pouch, and a scroll from a large box on the counter that ran along the back wall of the room.

Elsie gave the wolf who'd offended her a long look and moved to the center of the large room. "Reveal," she said and lifted her arms.

Runes appeared on the floor in a cross-shaped diagram inside of a circle. "Each of you take a position on a directional rune and remember where your position is. You'll," she pointed at Thaddeus who'd chosen the south rune, "will stand to the south of our witch." She pointed to Roan, "You to the west." She looked at the other two. "Once you have her centered, Blue, you'll have her hang this pouch from her neck, hold the crystal, and say what's on this scroll. You four will stand firm in your area of protection." She turned in a circle. "No matter what happens, you must not waiver."

The Witch reached up and pulled a long crude dagger from thin air. She kept the point of the dagger high, closed her eyes, and whispered under her breath, pushing power into the room. The runes on the floor began to glow. Blue magic flowed from the tip of the dagger down to the Witch, into the floor through the diagram and traveled to where the wolves stood.

The blue magic ran up their legs and pulsated through their bodies. The four threw their heads back at once, arms out at their sides, palms up. Their backs arched and stiffened as if they were being electrocuted. The Witch continued chanting until the magic flowed back from the four wolves, through the runes on which they stood, traveling along the diagram from where it had originated on the floor. The glowing blue ran back into the circle in a rush to return to the Witch's body. The Witch held the dagger toward the ceiling and her head fell back. "*Solicete porlo viem.*"

Anton and Thaddeus fell to their knees.

"You will now have a measure of influence over her. What this means is she will not perceive you as dangerous. She won't know why, but she will trust you. I have no way of knowing how much of her own magic has come in and how effective this spell will be. It's specific to her alone."

"As soon as you can pull yourselves together, you need to leave. We fear you may reach her too late," Max said.

The wolves nodded in agreement.

"Anything else?" Alicaster Blue asked him.

"Yes, the closest body of water to her location that still carries enough Earth Magic for this spell is an Ancient Lake a couple of hours northwest. You'll need to travel there to perform the ritual," Max instructed.

"Alicaster Blue is in charge." Max looked down at Anton. "He is your leader in my stead."

The Wolves filed out and one by one loaded up in the truck.

Elsie stepped up to stand next to Max.

"Are we too late?" Max mumbled.

Elsie shrugged. "If we are, we wasted the last three hundred years."

"You wasted the last three hundred years."

She wrapped her hand around his muscular arm and leaned her temple against it.

"Indeed, Wolf. Indeed."

Chapter 11

Eat rosemary to reduce inflammation and to help with problematic

digestive issues.

I stood in the refrigerator doorway, staring into the cold box,

not really seeing the contents. Another nightmare had

awoken me, and once again, another storm raged outside.

Lightning flashed, and the building shook, as sweat ran down

the back of my neck. The loud boom that followed was

deafening.

What was up with these summer storms? I grabbed a can of

flavored water from the refrigerator and slammed the door

shut as another flash lit up my small living room. My fingers

were tingling again, and I couldn't shake the nervous energy

that hummed through my body. I held the cold can against

the side of my neck and rolled my head.

The coolness of the can helped bring me focus. I caught a

flash out of the corner of my eye and jumped back, dropping

the can. Had lightning hit inside my condo? I looked to where I thought the bright light had occurred, and nothing was there. That was weird.

My fingers tingled painfully. It felt like the tips were going to burst. I'd convinced myself the new meds my doctor had me on must be causing this. It was the only change I'd made in the last few weeks just before all the crazy stuff started happening. These side effects were off the charts.

The tingling transitioned to burning, and I saw that my fingertips were now a weird shade of blue. Shoot. I'd heard of people losing appendages due to poor circulation from diabetes, but I'd always thought it was a gradual thing. I walked quickly back into the kitchen, turned on the facet, and thrust my hands under the cool water.

And that was when it all went south for me.

Blue and green sparks flew in every direction knocking me on my butt. The storm outside picked up its intensity, and a branch scraped my living room window, hard.

Something landed loudly on the roof making me jump. I crab-crawled backward, trying to get away from the sparks, but they seemed to be following me. It took longer than it should have for me to realize the sparks were coming from me. That's why I couldn't get away from them. I stopped scooting, sat on my rear, and moved my hands in front of my face. The sparks were shooting out of my fingers, like small blue and green sparklers. I let out a little sob and shook them. It didn't help. All it did was to send the sparks flying all over the living room and my coffee table. A few landed on my fluffy white throw blanket and created a puff of blue smoke.

I stopped shaking my hands, for fear of burning my condo down, when there was a bright flash followed by the low rumble of thunder that caught my attention. Another bang on the roof this time so hard, it knocked plaster off the ceiling and the lights flickered.

Great. Now not only was I about to not-so-spontaneously combust, but my house was going to get creamed by a storm, and to top it all off, the power was about to go out. I jumped to my feet and ran to the bedroom, ignoring the sparks that went everywhere my hands did.

I pulled out my ready-go-bag and began shoving into it the things I needed, like my diabetes medication and my iPhone charger. I stuffed my iPad and its charger in, too, and ran to my dresser, grabbing several pairs of undies and some clean T-shirts, along with a couple of pairs of jeans. I dropped to my knees and pulled out the drawer that held the pendant. I knew with my entire being I wasn't leaving it behind if I had to leave my house because of the storm. I removed it from the box I'd had it stored in, and for the very first time since receiving it, I placed it around my neck and tucked it under my shirt. As soon as it touched my skin, a charge ran through my body, and a branch came through my window, scaring the crap out of me and spurring me back into action.

I screamed and ran for my desk in the living room. I found the backpack that served as my purse. I flipped through my small filing cabinet until I reached the file that held my passport, birth certificate, and social security card. My heart was pounding in my chest as I pulled it out and crammed the file into my backpack. I zipped it up, slipping my arms through the straps.

Back at my bedroom, I saw what looked like twenty black snakes slithering into my bedroom off of the large branch that had crashed through my window. They were black, with ash and smoke misting off of them, with bright green eyes. One of them fixated on me and hissed, baring its long deadly fangs. I grabbed my bag, screamed again, and ran for the door. I know what I'm about to say next will be unbelievable, but as I was running for my front door, a shadow claw reached out and caught my ankle, tripping me. My bag flew closer to the door but was still open and several vials of my insulin rolled out and one by one exploded.

"What the f..." I screamed.

"*Run, you fool!*" a woman said in my head.

"What?" I asked no one. Looking around the empty room, I scooted myself closer to my bag. I scooped up what I could as I watched the snake things slither out of my room toward me. *"Run now or die!"* the woman's voice urged.

I decided to listen to my newfound inner voice and gathered my bag, slid my feet into my rubber boots that stayed by my door, picked up my keys, and flung my front door open so I could make a run for Ol' Bessie.

The violence of the storm that greeted me was like nothing I'd ever experienced before, and I'd lived there my entire life. The force threw me backwards into my condo and ripped my go-bag from my hands. I managed to stop my backward motion by clinging to the doorway and pulled myself outside and onto the stairwell. I clung to the railing as I half slid, half ran down the steps.

That's when I realized no one else in my building was awake. I ran to Old Man Miller's door.

"Mr. Miller," I screamed, just before a large green ball of flame hit his front door as I raised my fist to bang on it. I watched in horror as the ball melted Mr. Miller's door, and green fire shot out from his condo.

"No!" I screamed and attempted to run into the flames. Strong hands grabbed my upper arms from behind and pulled me back against a hard chest.

"You can't save him now, love. You can't save any of them."

I cried out and looked up into the handsome face of Rolfe, the fortune teller. Only now he looked different. His eyes weren't arctic blue anymore but glowing blue. He had long fangs overlapping his lower lip. I looked down at his hands that were still holding onto me and saw that dagger-shaped clear claws protruded his long fingers.

He watched me and followed my eyes down to his hands. I looked back up into his face with big eyes and screamed.

I fought the hold he had on me unsuccessfully until he joined in the screaming and flung us both away from the new ball of green flame as it hit the building that was once my home. We landed on the asphalt, and I cried out. My neighbors were burning in their sleep, and there wasn't anything I could do about it! A sob escaped, and my gaze turned to the man who'd saved me.

I scrambled to get up and away from this new version of Rolfe. I'd made it to my feet when movement from my condo caught my eye. I watched in horror as the snake creatures slithered down the stairs and side of my building at an alarming speed and seemed to be heading directly toward us. I ran for Ol' Bessie with all I had in me. I fumbled for my keys before I even reached her and hit my key fob to gain quick entrance. I jumped in and was relieved when I felt my backpack on as I tried to sit back. I'd lost my go-bag, but at least I still had my purse.

I released one strap and pulled it around to the front of my body as Rolfe climbed into the passenger side and yelled, "Drive, girl! Drive now!"

I didn't even think about the fact that he had claws and fangs. I only knew that he was just as scared as I was and wanted away from the snakes and green fire too.

I turned my sweet girl over, and she started right up.

"That green flame better not touch my Ol' Bessie!" I said as I slammed her into reverse and stomped on the gas pedal.

"It will melt anything it touches," Rolfe said.

I whipped the car out of my parking spot and shifted it into drive, without even coming to a complete stop.

"What?" I asked. "It'll melt Bessie?"

Rolfe's face planted into the passenger window when I swerved to keep a ball of green flame from hitting my sweet old ride.

"We must escape it, or it will kill us."

"I'll do one better," I mumbled and said loudly, "I want all the green flames and fire to stop." I looked in the rearview mirror as pain pierced my left eye and traveled straight through my brain. "Ugh!" I yelled as I watched the green flames vanish as if they were never there.

Rolfe swiveled in his seat to watch out the back window and let out a sigh of relief.

I slowed the escape, and he said, "What are you doing? Keep going!"

"The green flame is gone. Crisis averted," I said, and rolled almost to a stop. "I need to call nine-one-one."

"You only stopped the fire. All the other creatures that were sent after you are still there!"

And as if on cue, a black snake dropped onto my hood and used its face to try and bust through the windshield at me. Its beady little green glowing eyes fixated on my face as it slammed its head over and over against my windshield.

"Get off my car!" I yelled and no sooner was the command out of my mouth when the snake was whipped away. My fingers tingled painfully.

Panting, I looked at Rolfe.

"What are you?" I asked in a quiet scream. My voice was going to be gone if I didn't get a handle on my reaction to the terror.

He squinted at me and asked, "What do you see when you look upon me?"

"Fangs, claws, glowing eyes." I rolled my eyes toward him to make sure. "Yep. That's what I see."

"Did you see me this way when you visited me at the fortune tellers?" he asked.

I squinted, the pain in my head was intense. "You aren't the fortune teller, are you?"

"No, I am not."

"I knew it!"

"Did you know it then?" he asked, watching me closely. Like he could tell if I lied.

"Nope. Then you looked like a tall, fair-haired, well-dressed guy." I looked at him. "Not now. Now you look like some kind of well-dressed hell demon."

"Watch your tongue, Witch." Goosebumps rolled over my skin.

"Why'd you call me that?" I whispered.

"Because it is precisely what you are. You obviously don't know it...yet. But you, my dear, are, without a doubt, a witch. The ends of your hair glow when you use your magic. Every witch has a tell. Yours is your hair."

"No, I'm not! No, it isn't!"

This was the second time someone recently had referred to me as a witch, and it was starting to piss me off. I grabbed the end of my hair, and yes, it was whiter than normal. It wasn't glowing.

Rolfe looked at me with hard eyes. "Never deny who you are. You have the gift of persuasion, and your powers can be used against even you. If you say you aren't a witch, when, in fact, you are, there could be dire consequences."

Goosebumps landed on the goosebumps that were already taking up space on my skin.

"What do you mean?"

"I mean every natural being in this realm and others can see your magical signature. You're a walking bullseye, and you don't even know it."

"What..." I didn't know what to say. This was too much. Magical signatures? Realms?

"You need to learn to measure your words." He brushed dirt from his pressed black slacks. "What is different from the last time we met?" He shifted to get a good look at me. "Where's the pendant?"

"I'm wearing it."

"Is this the first time?"

"Yes, I put it on when I was escaping my house."

"Hhhmm, did you by chance cleanse it?"

"No, I just stuck it back in my drawer."

"Why didn't you follow my instructions?"

"Because I didn't realize they were instructions. I thought they were suggestions. If I had any inkling creatures would come out of the tree to attack me and green flame balls would melt my building, I'd have paid more attention!"

"We'll need to test the theory when we stop."

"I don't even know where we're going!" I screeched. I was about at the end of my rope.

"I think the pendant is an amulet and it's protecting you."

"It isn't doing a very good job!"

"I'm curious if they will be able to find you if you're wearing it. I believe it gives you the ability to see beings for what they really are and not the glamour they show you."

"So, you're saying, normal you was a glamour?"

"Yes. That was a human version of me."

"And this," I waved a hand in his general direction, "is the real you?"

"That's about it."

"Then I ask again, what are you?" I pushed power into my voice and looked down. Sure enough, the ends of my hair glowed bright white. Danggit.

"I'm Vampire."

I gripped the steering wheel and stomped on the brakes as hard as I could.

"Get out!" I shouted forcefully. If he was right, he wouldn't be able to keep himself from doing what I asked.

He opened the door. "You need me. I'm not going to hurt you. I've never seen a real witch before." He stepped out of Ol' Bessie. "Your kind has been extinct since I became." He stood on the road inside the door frame. "You'll be killed before you even get a chance to be, if you don't have help of some kind." He was speaking quickly. I'm sure he realized how close I was to driving away and leaving him there.

I didn't want to reply, or rescind my command, but I also needed to know more about what was going on. He was my only link to the crazy crap that was flying around me. Keeping in mind that I'd just suffered an attack from tree shadow snakes, I realized I needed him, unfortunately.

"I command you never to harm me," I said with as much force as I could manage, the pounding in my head intensified.

"I swear on the House of Lore, and all that reside in it, I will not lay a hand against you."

"Okay, I didn't understand some of that, but we can talk about it later. Climb back in. Let's get on the road."

"As you command."

I looked at him. I wasn't sure if he was making fun of me. I scowled at him for good measure. "You will *never* suck my blood."

Rolfe smiled at me and said, "I will not suck your blood... unless you ask me to."

"You will never suck my blood." If magic powers, green flames, and deadly red-eyed snakes weren't enough, now I had to worry about bloodsuckers!

Chapter 12

Wear rose quartz to stabilize energy and use it as a

conduit for love potions.

I drove Rolfe to the fortune teller's shop, because we didn't

know where else to go. I had a load of questions, but I also

needed to eat or I would be a mess in a very short time.

Seeing him as a Vampire was scary and made me not want to

look at him so I kept my face averted while driving.

Luckily, we didn't suffer any additional attacks, and I was able

to park right in front of the shop.

"The sun will be up soon, my love, and I'm afraid I won't be

able to help you." Rolfe opened the front door and closed it

behind us. "Come back here where it's safe."

I followed him past the main front room I'd been in before

and through a thick set of curtains to a rather large kitchen

and living area.

"So, Vampires really do sleep during the day?"

He nodded. "We are our most vulnerable during the day. If we are found and taken outdoors in the sunlight, we turn to ash."

"Can't you just stay indoors?"

"I'm afraid it doesn't work that way. We aren't animated during the daylight hours. It's part of the agreement for our immortality."

I wandered around his place and realized it was very nice.

"What happened to the fortune teller?"

"She owed the House of Lore a debt, and I was sent to collect."

I stopped and focused on Rolfe. "Is she dead?"

He shrugged his shoulders.

"Is that a yes, or no?" I asked. "Answer me."

"Yes." He seemed surprised by his own answer and lowered his eyes to me.

"Tell me, did you kill her?" I asked and this time was intentional about my words.

"Yes," he snarled at me.

"How is it possible that Vampires are real?"

"There is always a grain of truth in everything you hear."

"This isn't a grain of truth. This is the whole truth. There are books, television shows, comics, and movies about Vampires, for heaven's sake. You're right out in the open, and we still don't believe you exist!"

He shrugged his shoulders. "I must retire soon."

I needed to know as much as I could, and honestly, for whatever reason, I didn't feel like I was under threat, so I continued my questioning.

"How did you find me?"

He shrugged his shoulders again. "I'm a tracker."

"What does that mean?"

"It means if I can catch the scent of a human or other .... individual, I can always find them."

"Always?"

"Always."

"Why did you save me?"

He laughed. "Are you kidding? You're a witch. Do you have any idea how much you're worth? The bidding war alone will be the biggest ever known to Vampire! I'll bring great honor to my house. My rewards will be life-changing. Your capture might even improve my rank."

"You were going to sell me?" I was starting to dislike this Vampire, even if he did save me from the green fire and snakes. "Like human trafficking?"

"Humans are aplenty." He waved his hand. "They throw themselves at us as offerings. Their puny lives are barely worth mentioning. Cattle to us, they are." He smiled.

I squinted at him. He was a predator, through and through.

"So, if you'd managed to capture me, what would you have done?" I asked.

"I have captured you, and I plan to hand you over to the court."

Chills ran over my skin. He didn't have me, I told myself. I had him. Yes, that's how I would approach this. I had him, and he needed to answer my questions. I smiled, and he narrowed his glowing eyes at me.

"The court?"

"Yes, each Vampire house has its own court and congress."

"Why am I valuable?"

"I told you. You're a witch. The only one I've met. There aren't any more of you left…" He stopped talking, and I got the impression there was more he wanted to say.

"What makes you think I'm a witch?"

"You glow … with it…" His words were slurring, and he'd begun swaying back and forth. I pulled back the curtain to see that soft morning sunlight was streaming through the front window.

"Do you need to rest?"

"Yes." He moved clumsily to a door and threw it open. "I must get to my room below, or I shall be a corpse lying vulnerable throughout the day."

I nodded. I certainly didn't want to have to deal with a dead-looking Rolfe.

"Go on, then. I'll see you tonight."

He looked at me and smiled. He knew and I knew I wouldn't be there when he woke.

"I'll find you. You won't be able to shake me."

"Rolfe?"

"Yes, my love?" He opened his bedroom door.

"You will never come looking for me." I rubbed my temples.

"No..."

"You won't even remember me." I closed my eyes; the light from the lamp was too painful to take in.

"Cassandra..."

"Starting now. Go to bed, Rolfe, and thank you for saving me. Now, when you wake, you won't remember anything about me, my condo, or this night."

Without a word, he turned and disappeared through the door that led down a long flight of stairs into pitch-black darkness. I closed the door behind him and took a deep breath. I rummaged around the small kitchen and soon discovered there wasn't any food, I guess Vampires didn't need to eat, like us lowly humans. I remembered my backpack was still in Ol' Bessie, and I'd have a couple of emergency protein bars there.

I needed to figure out what my next plan of action was. Could I go back to my condo? Surely now that the sun was up, I'd be safe. But how would I explain what had happened? No one would believe me. They'd think I started the fire if I tried to tell them green-eyed snakes and shadow claws were involved. I'd lose all credibility. They'd rightfully think I'd lost my mind and probably think I'd burned the place down.

I caught my breath. Old Man Miller was gone. I saw his home explode with my own eyes. I covered my mouth to hold in the scream that threatened to slip out. If I didn't get a handle on myself, I'd never be able to figure out what the next right move was.

First things first, I needed to get some insulin and food. Once I knew I was thinking clearly, I could sort my feelings, wrap my head around the fact that Vampires existed, and make a plan. Yes, that's it. I loved making plans.

The first plan, retrieve my backpack and take care of my health. Then, and only then, would I be able to think clearly enough to decide what my next course of action was.

I marched to the door, unlocked it, and threw it open.

Chapter 13

Write the things that worry you the most on a scrap of old paper and toss it

into a fire. Watch as your fears go up in flames, and rejoice.

"**W**e're at the location but there's no sign of her," Alicaster

Blue said into his phone. "There was a magical battle to be

sure. Several fatalities, three humans and a cat. All occupants

of the same building as our witch. The human authorities are

blaming it on an accidental fire."

He looked around at the human crews that were still cleaning

up. The sun hadn't fully risen but was just about to crest the

horizon.

"They aren't even questioning the tree branches that are

sticking out of the witch's apartment." Alicaster Blue swiveled

his head to the tree line and focused on the two trees that

were missing rather large sections. "The trees are easily a

hundred feet away from her residence."

The four wolves stood at the edge of the complex parking lot with their backs to the wooded park. They appeared to be nothing more than large, dark-haired men dressed in black to the humans who bustled around the devastation. Some say Alicaster Blue got his name because his hair was so black, it was blue, or maybe it was because of his piercing blue eyes. But either way, along with his perpetual five o'clock shadow, he was a devilishly handsome wolf.

Anton broke off from the wolf pack and headed to the demolished apartment. Alicaster Blue tilted his head toward Thaddeus to follow Anton.

"Hell! Damn! I'll alert Elsie. She'll have to scry and pick her up again," Max responded.

"Max, there's something else." Alicaster Blue lowered his voice and turned toward Roan who was standing with him at the edge of the wooded park. "I smell vampire."

Roan nodded in agreement to the phone conversation with their Alpha.

"Vampire? How many?" Max asked.

"I scent one," Alicaster Blue replied.

Roan nodded again.

"Can you follow its scent?" Max was enraged. He hated bloodsuckers like any wolf worth his weight would.

"Yes, but it's intermingled with the witch. I believe they might be traveling together."

"By force?"

"Too hard to tell. The place reeks of her fear, but with this amount of damage, I can't imagine she wouldn't be afraid."

"If she went with it willingly, she couldn't know how much danger she's in."

"I thought the same. By the looks of her apartment and what happened here, she barely escaped with her life." He dropped his head. "She'd have been able to defeat the magic that was waged against her, if she'd known who she was."

"Now we have the vampires to contend with."

"At least this one."

"Can you determine if it's male or female?"

"I cannot. I'm afraid my contact, and therefore knowledge, of the leech population is limited to the Blood Wars. When I catch up to it, I'll kill it."

"Blue..."

"When I catch it, I kill it," he repeated himself.

"I understand. Some transgressions aren't to be forgotten. Get on her trail right away and check in when you have something. I'll apprise Elsie of the situation. She was able to scry her once, surely she'll be able to do it again."

"*Veek*," Alicaster Blue said to his Alpha.

"*Veek ent*," Max disconnected the call.

"Blue, I picked up the scent of the bloodsucker too. The witch is being hunted by bloodsuckers." Roan clenched his fists. He'd heard the stories of how the Vampire had worked against the witches during the dark ages. First driving them from Europe, and when Europe wasn't enough, they instigated and influenced the hysteria that resulted in the witch burnings in the New World.

"I believe they are traveling together."

"What!" Roan hit the base of the tree he was standing near, fluttering its leaves to the ground.

"We are to continue tracking the scent. Max will ask Elsie to scry once more for us."

"I've got something," Anton said, approaching the group. He held a partially burned bag and a small box with a large magical presence humming from it.

"The contents of this box was magical, and it's witch magic," he said and held up the small box.

He switched hands and held up the bag. "This has her scent all over it. Including the stench of fear. I can track this."

"I'm not getting Vampire from the bag." Alicaster Blue sniffed.

"Nope. It's her." Bringing the burnt bag to his nose, Anton took in her scent and rolled his eyes back. "She smells delicious."

Thaddeus snatched the bag out of Anton's hand. "Don't imprint on her before you've even spoken to her."

Anton's large canines were prominent in his predatory smile. "Too late."

Thaddeus stepped forward. "We have to stay focused on spelling her into her magic and then back to Thornwood. Besides, every wolf who wants one gets a shot at a witch."

"I'm not stopping you, old man." Anton slapped Thaddeus on the back and leaned toward his head. "But I'm not waiting for you, either," he growled and nipped at Thaddeus's ear.

"You little pelt!" Thaddeus roared and lunged for Anton, who stepped back quickly as Alicaster Blue grabbed Thaddeus by the back of his shirt, halting his forward motion.

"That's enough. The fate of us all rests on our shoulders. You can fight over the girl *after* we've saved her species from extinction."

"Some of us never had the luxury of knowing what it's like to have a witch," Anton growled.

Alicaster Blue released the growling Thaddeus and stepped toward Anton.

"You don't have a witch; they have you. Quit thinking you're getting a new girlfriend. Witches are very different from humans. Even witches who think they're human are still witches. It'll serve you well to remember that."

He stepped back and addressed the group. "There are thirteen witches if everything goes according to plan. There are roughly thirty wolves. That's only two wolves for each witch. Not enough to keep them protected." He met the eye of each wolf. "Witches are a lot of trouble and work. Don't let Elsie fool you. She and Max have been at it for centuries."

"Are you bowing out of becoming a guardian, Blue?" Roan asked.

Alicaster Blue grinned and flashed his canines. "I'd never miss out on a chance to be a guardian again. It was the most fun I've ever had. Right up until the very end."

"A vampire ups our game. Our window just folded in on itself. We need to find her now," Roan said. "Anton, you got a clear grasp on her trail?"

Anton nodded and stepped forward. "Let's go before the sun reaches the sky and while the trail is still fresh. I'm in the back."

The black truck roared away from the parking lot with the driver and passenger in the cab, and two giant wolves in the bed of the truck.

Anton ran to the left of the bed, and Roan made a sharp left. And so, on it went as they followed the scent the witch and vampire left. They'd been at it for more than an hour when they came upon a large older model suburban with strong magic; the scent of the witch ended with it. Anton and Thaddeus quickly dressed while Roan and Alicaster Blue checked out the vehicle.

"She can't be far," Roan whispered. The sun was almost in the sky, and the human world was awakening, but it was still early.

"This is a shopping area. Everything is closed. What's around here that would cause them to stop?"

"Could a fortune teller fit the bill?" Thaddeus asked as he approached pointing over his pack members. Three heads looked up to the sign above the door to the shop the suburban was parked in front of.

"Yeah, that might be it," Roan replied.

"I smell Vampire," Thaddeus growled.

Alicaster Blue looked into the sky. "Doesn't matter. Sun's up. It won't be animated. It'll hide itself somewhere safe. The real question is; did he take the witch with him?"

The fortune teller's shop door whipped open.

"Get away from my car!" a female yelled from the doorway. The four wolves immediately stepped back away from the vehicle. The woman slipped out of the store and closed the door.

"Do not go into that shop." She grimaced and pointed at the door. "There's nothing of value to you anyway." She moved slowly to a vehicle parked at the curb.

"I can't move," Thaddeus said.

"Stay where you are until I'm gone, and then you can go about your business." She rubbed her temples and made a move toward her car. She stopped, seemed to think of something that had her add, "and don't break into anyone else's car and don't steal stuff anymore... Unless you're dying or starving, then do what you must." She shook her head and muttered to herself, "Do no harm."

"Witch," Anton growled. She stopped mid-step and looked at the handsome 'man.'

"We've come to save you. We were sent to serve as your guardians by Elsie, the Last Witch," Thaddeus said while she stared at Anton.

"Why did you call me a witch?" she asked Anton, ignoring Thaddeus.

"That's what you are. You are the first of the Thirteen to awaken. We are your guardians. We've come to protect you from grave danger." He tried to take a step toward her but found himself unable to move.

"Do you know what's going on with me?" she asked.

They answered in unison, "Yes."

That's when the wolves noticed tears streaming down her face. Anton tilted his head and watched her. He didn't know witches could cry.

The witch turned her gaze to Thaddeus. "Tell me."

"You were attacked by dark magic that is trying to murder you before you fully realize your power." He looked at Alicaster Blue. "I had to tell her that."

Thaddeus watched the young woman drop to rest her rear on her heels and began to sob while holding her head in her hands.

"I thought I was losing my mind. How could that have happened? I mean, I know what I saw... and the fortune teller isn't a fortune teller at all, but instead a vampire? What the heck is happening?" She rambled on, some of what she said the wolves couldn't make out, but they got the gist that she was experiencing an epic meltdown.

"Vampires are the reason Witches are almost extinct," Alicaster Blue growled.

The woman's head whipped up, and she stopped crying. She looked back over her shoulder at the shop she'd just exited. "No."

"Yes," he hissed at her.

"Technically, humans persecuting the witches for centuries is the reason witches are almost extinct, but Vampire drove them to it," Roan said quietly.

"Why can't I move?" Thaddeus asked.

"I, well... I kind of have influence over people, and objects, it seems... with my words," she sniffed.

"Ah. How long have you known this gift?"

"A couple of weeks. It just started one night and never stopped. A woman called me a witch and gave me a pendant." She pulled her crystal out from under her shirt to show them. "It was driving me absolutely insane, but then when I put it on, it allowed me to see Rolfe for his true self." She looked around the group of men. "You all look fine, but you have something extra about you."

"We are wolves."

"Anton!" Thaddeus shouted.

"Wolves?"

"We are born to a wolf mother, but after our twelfth full moon, we gain the ability to shift into man form too. Those of us who don't get eaten by the wolf pack manage to find each other and survive."

"That's brutal!" she cried.

"That's nature. Only the strongest can become a guardian."

"You say you're here to protect me?" She looked at all four men.

"We are. But we must first take you to the Ancient Lake and perform your awakening spell to bring you into your magic," Roan said.

"Magic? That's what this is?" She looked at her hands. "The finger tingles and sparks were magic?"

"I need to know more about the vampire you were with, Witch," Alicaster Blue interjected.

"Our mission is to get the witch, do the spell, and get her back to Thornwood before those opposed find her and kill her. We aren't side-tracking and putting the first of the Thirteen at risk to kill a vamp," Thaddeus whispered to Alicaster Blue.

"Rolfe saved my life," she said quietly. "I can't let you hurt him. Even if he was going to sell me to his court."

The wolves growled, and Cassandra shivered. Something about them made her feel like she wasn't all alone. Maybe they could be trusted?

A car drove by, and another parked behind the suburban.

"Look, I admit I don't have a clue what's happening. I haven't had any sleep, I have a job to get to, and I need to figure my condo out, so while this has been interesting I have somewhere I've got to be. I would like to see you after work, if that's possible. I have a ton of questions."

"You can't go to work," Thaddeus said. "That's the first place they'll strike next."

"No! I have a job I have to finish. It's my company. If I flake on this job, I won't ever be able to find work in this town again!" she yelled.

"You don't need to find work in this town. Because you won't be here!" Thaddeus shouted. "Let us go immediately. Every moment we spend debating is one more moment they have to track us down and strike!"

She wrapped her arms around her knees and put her head down and rocked. The wolves looked at each other. This witch was not behaving in any way how they thought a witch, who was supposed to be one of the Thirteen, would behave. This witch was acting like a human female.

"I thought you said witches didn't act like humans?" Anton mumbled to Alicaster Blue.

"I've never seen this before," he replied to Anton and turned his attention back to the witch on the sidewalk and yelled, "Elsie! We need you!"

The hand that The Last Witch had embedded a crystal into grew warm and began glowing. Alicaster Blue's arm thrust forward, and an image projected from his palm about three feet in height.

Elsie was there in hologram form. "Blue, you summoned me?"

"What the...." the human witch muttered.

"Ah. I see you have the first of the Thirteen. Fine work. Hurry and open her magic so she can control herself. Then come straight back to Thornwood Manor."

"She wants to go to work, Elsie," Alicaster Blue said.

The Last Witch turned her translucent form to address the new witch.

"Cassandra, I know this is very confusing, but you must trust us. We are yours. I am your sister. These wolves are here to protect you from now until the end of eternity... if you wish it."

Cassandra lifted her head and stared open-mouthed at the hologram.

Chapter 14

Ancient lakes can be found all over the world. If you get a chance to travel to one try to do so during a full moon. Remember to take your crystals for some extra juice!

There stood the coolest-looking chick I'd ever seen in a

three-foot projection. Star Wars style. Princess Leia had
nothing on this chick. The color and clarity of the projection
was intense and off the charts fantastic.
Admittedly, this was my first three-foot projection... so other
than the movies, I didn't have anything else to compare it to.
But she was awesome! She had long silver-white braids with
the upper section wrapped in a loose bun on top of her head.
Several Nordic-style tattoos adorned her face, three across her
forehead, one under each eye, one on her chin, and down
both sides of her neck. It looked awesome on her. She was
wearing some kind of light blue sheath dress, was barefoot,

and had a wad of wrapped crystal jewelry around her neck, wrists, and ankles.

But the coolest part was how her eyes seemed to *glow*.

The men who insisted on referring to themselves as wolves seemed just as transfixed by her as I was. Then she called me out by name, and I felt a shudder work through my body. She was my people. I could feel it in every fiber of my being. My entire life, I'd always been outside looking in. Never really fitting in anywhere. Sure, I found my way, and sure, I'd even made some friends. But I always knew I was different. I'd learned how to assimilate, but never truly felt like I belonged. But now I *knew*.

I knew I belonged with her. I could *feel* it. That frightened me more than anything else that had happened thus far. And that was saying something, because a lot of crazy stuff had gone down.

"How do I know this isn't some kind of spell you're casting on me?" I asked her and wondered how tall she was in real life.

"You'd know. Just like you know in your soul of souls I am your sister. You can feel our magic speaking to each other, can't you?"

The weird thing was, I could. I could feel my 'magic' running through my limbs like it was getting ready to welcome an old friend home from a long journey. My inner being was excited.

She'd never been anything but fearful. Now I could feel the elation streaming through my body.

"We don't have any time to waste. I fear there are trackers pursuing you, even as we speak."

"I need to wrap my head around this. It's so much to take in. Where exactly do you want me to go?"

"You've used your influence on the wolves when you asked your questions so you know who they are, and why I've sent them. You must first travel to the Ancient Lake, perform the awakening spell that will bring you into your magic, then come directly to Thornwood Manor," she replied. "We have so little time and so much to do."

"Where is the Ancient Lake?" I asked. "Why do I need to go there first?"

"It's part of the spell. It's the closest body of magical water to you. You need to be able to defend yourself and help your potential guardians keep you alive until you reach me. Here, you'll be as safe as you can be anywhere in the world."

I shook my head and stood. "I can't leave my plaster unfinished. Don't the bad guys only strike at night? It's full sun. I can go, finish my work, collect my pay, and then I still need to figure out my condo. It's a wreck. I have to contact my insurance, deal with the HOA ...so much to do."

"The vilest creatures can only strike under the cover of night. However, that doesn't mean you're safe during the day. There are plenty of creatures who enjoy full sunlight who would love nothing more than to strike the first of the Thirteen down."

I didn't know what she was referring to; I just knew that my agenda and theirs didn't line up. I needed to handle my stuff so I could keep living the life I had worked so hard to build. Why was I even considering going with these people? Also, my head hurt so bad, all I wanted to do was close my eyes and shut out the world.

"I'm sorry, I think you've got the wrong girl. There's just no way I can be a witch." It was too ridiculous to consider. In an attempt to get a handle on reality, I looked up at the now bright sky and squinted from the pain. Something was up there.

I tried to focus and pointed at several large black birds that were circling above. High enough that I wasn't worried about them pooping on my face, but it was still curious.

"What's happening?" the witch Elsie's hologram asked. I looked at her projection and she said, "I can feel a build-up of dark magic... what's coming? Can you see anything?"

I could feel it too. Like the brewing of a heavy storm so large, you could feel its electricity in the air. A bird shrieked. It sounded angry. I looked up to see that the circling blackbirds had tripled in numbers and seemed to be closer.

"They've found us," one of the men said in a low growl.

"Cassandra, you need to release the wolves now and get out of there," the hologram witch shouted at me.

I felt the push she sent with her words. I knew she was trying to influence me, but after the way I woke up, I certainly didn't want to have to contend with whatever these birds had in mind. They were closer now, and I got a good look at them. They were scarily large and black, with wicked beaks and talons.

"Those don't look like regular crows," I mumbled.

"They aren't crows. They're Death Ravens," one of the men yelled. "Release us now!"

"Cassandra, free the wolves this instant!" the hologram shrieked, and nothing on the face of this earth could have stopped me from saying, "You're all free to move at your own discretion."

The men jumped to action, and Elsie's hologram disappeared. The largest of the bunch, and believe me, they were all large, but this one had jet black hair, ran towards me. Before I knew what he was about, he had his shoulder in my stomach, and I was lifted fireman style as he stood and ran.

I grabbed hold of the back of his shirt to balance myself and peered up. The circling birds were tripled in size from the last time I looked and were getting closer. Their ear-piercing screech reverberated against my eardrums. On closer inspection, the birds weren't only growing in numbers but also seemed to be growing in size individually. Like, each bird was getting bigger.

And they were coming for us.

"Run faster," I yelled, and luckily this seemed to help, because the man who was carrying me not only picked up speed, but he passed his friends with me bouncing around over his shoulder.

I waved at one of the surprised guys as we passed. The smarty pants in me couldn't resist.

"Does your influence work on animals?" the man carrying me yelled.

"It worked on inanimate objects, so I would think so," I yelled back.

We reached a large black four-door truck and stopped. The other men arrived just as he whipped open the door, and I was flung inside. From there, I was forced to scoot or get sat on.

"Do you think you could make them back off?" my rescuer shouted as the truck was pummeled by the birds throwing their bodies against it, just as the other men slammed the doors closed behind them. The birds hit the truck so hard, it rocked from the impact. The sound level inside the truck was deafening, so I covered my ears.

"I can try," I yelled back.

"Focus on the birds and direct your words toward them," he shouted.

It was easy to concentrate on the birds. I really did want them to go away. Actually, it was impossible not to concentrate on them. They were after all committing mass suicide against the truck we were in.

"Stop hitting the truck!" I yelled and closed my eyes. The pain in my head was sharp and intense. Also, I didn't want to see what would happen next if it didn't work.

The noise stopped immediately, and the inside of the truck went still. I opened my eyes to find the windows filled with large black birds with red beady eyes staring at me. Hundreds of eyes focused on me at once. I could feel their malice. I rubbed my arms where goosebumps had taken up permanent residence. If they ever got a hold of me, I was a goner. There were so many of them. They were at least four deep, not a pinprick of sunlight could make its way through the sea of black.

"Get this bucket moving!" the passenger shouted.

The truck squealed away from the curb. The windshield immediately cleared of the birds once we started moving, but a number of them were able to keep up for a few minutes. I watched out the back window until the last one dropped off.

I was sitting in the back between the black-haired guy who'd carried me and the guy with a beard and pretty green eyes.

"I'm Cassandra." I smiled at green eyes.

He smiled back and said to the men, "Grab and go. Didn't I say the best way to get her was to grab her and go?"

"I'm Anton," he said to me and stuck his hand out. "I'd like to formally submit my request to be your guardian. And unlike old man Blue here," he pointed to the man who'd carried me, "I'll let you climb on my back next time you need to be run off with." He raised his eyebrows and smiled another toothy grin. That's when I noticed his large canine teeth.

They weren't long and razor-sharp like Rolfe's were once I could truly see him, but still, they were larger and sharper than normal and looked lethal. I must have been staring for a while because he ran his thick tongue over one of them and said, "Wanna touch it?"

I looked at his handsomely rugged face and decided I didn't want my fingers anywhere near his sharp teeth. Something inside of me just knew he'd take any opportunity to take a bite.

"Next to you is Alicaster Blue, we call him Blue for short, or sometimes we call him Old Man."

I studied the man sitting on the other side of me. Anton referred to him as an old man, but he didn't look any older than Anton, in my opinion. Blue, he'd called him, had jet back hair, an unshaven face, and beautiful blue eyes that seemed to look right through me.

"Thank you for saving me," I whispered.

He looked at me and grinned, showing the same large canine teeth. "Thank you for the boost. I've never run that fast in all my days."

"You call him an old man. Don't drag the rest of us into this," the front passenger said and smiled at me.

Anton continued, "That's Roan, and our chauffeur is Thaddeus."

"Dial Max," Thaddeus, the driver, said to the car.

A disembodied female voice replied, "Dialing Max." And the interior of the truck filled with one ring before the call was answered.

"Is the witch with you?" was the greeting from the person on the other end.

"We've got her. Making our way to the Ancient Lake now," the driver answered.

"What happened?" Max asked.

"Birds. Death Ravens, to be precise," Blue said.

"Those are tough buggars. How did you get away?"

"The witch willed it," Thaddeus replied.

"She did, eh?" The man on the phone sounded like he was smiling.

"She commanded it, actually," Blue said, and I saw that he *was* smiling. What was up with all the happiness? Didn't we just get attacked by a bunch of creepy birds?

"We barely escaped the red-eyed devil birds. What is all the grinning about?" I asked everyone in the car.

The driver was the only one who didn't turn to stare at me.

"They had red eyes?" Blue growled.

"They had beady little glowing red eyes. How could you have missed that?" The memory of them made my stomach hurt. I turned as much as the seat belt would allow me to face him.

"Am I hearing this right?" Max asked.

"Did all of them have red eyes?" Blue had my full attention. He was so focused on me that chills ran over my arms.

I spoke slowly. "When I told them to stop hitting the truck, and they covered the windows with their bodies, they stared at us with their red glowing eyes. Did you guys not see their eyes?"

The men were still watching me closely.

"Witch, after you told them to stop hitting the truck, they vanished."

"No..." I shook my head.

"Red eyes mean the *magic maker* was able to see you, and capture the magical signature of Cassandra," the man on the phone said.

"Those were scouts," Blue growled next to me.

Chills ran over my skin again. "Am I seeing things now?" I asked.

"You saw what you weren't meant to see. It's unexpected that you'd have those capabilities before performing the *awakening*," Blue said while studying me. "Tell me about this vampire you were with."

I gave him the side-eye and asked, "why?"

"You weren't surprised when we told you about the vampire. In fact, you knew it was a vampire and went so far as to protect it during its non-animation."

"He is a "he" not an "it" and he saved my life!"

Chapter 15

When life becomes too much to handle, or you have an important decision to make, take your shoes off and dig your toes into the grass, dirt, or sand...Mother Earth recharges and brings clarity.

"If he saved your life, he only did it because it served him,"

Blue growled.

"How did you know he was Vampire?" Thaddeus asked, watching me in the rearview mirror.

"Well, I didn't the first time we met. He was a fortune teller I went to see about this pendant I was given." I pulled the crystal out of my shirt and held it up by the chain. "Someone slipped this to me and told me to "do no harm". When I went to return it, because I hadn't paid for it, she was gone."

"She?" Thaddeus asked.

"Yes, it was weird."

I spent the next few minutes recounting the story. I shared that the pendant was what enabled me to see Rolfe for who he truly was. That led to me recounting the morning I'd woken up from the night terror and found the new influence I had with my words. They asked questions, and I answered the best I could.

Honestly, it was a relief to have people to tell who didn't think I was crazy. Not only did they not think I was crazy, they actually believed me and had some pretty valuable input.

"What does the pendant look like?" Max asked over the truck phone.

"I'll take a picture and text it to you." Blue whipped out his phone, and I heard the camera function sound, and then the swish as it was sent off via text.

"If the pendant allowed her to see the Vampire..." Blue said.

"Rolfe," I interjected.

"...then it might be the reason she was able to see what wasn't meant for her with the Death Ravens." He leaned in to get a close-up look at the crystal. I had to fight myself not to jerk it out of his view.

"That actually makes more sense. But now the questions are; who gave her the pendant? How did they know Cassandra was one of the Thirteen? Are they the reason her magic came to her before the awakening ritual was performed? And what else does the pendant do?" Max asked.

"Wait, I left my backpack in Ol' Bessie! We need to go back," I said. "I'd like to at least notify my job that I won't be in today. I need my phone." The looks I got from the other occupants of the car had me expand, "Okay, the rest of the week."

"Never," Thaddeus said from behind the wheel.

"What?" I asked.

"You are never going back to work."

"Yes, I am." This guy was starting to piss me off.

"Cassandra," Max interrupted our argument, "Elsie wants to speak with you."

"Okay," I said, but gave the stink eye to the back of the head of the guy driving who thought he could boss me around. I looked at Anton next to me, and he grinned. I doubled down on my glare.

"Cassandra, the pendant you're wearing. Have you taken it off since putting it on last night?"

"Only for a brief moment back at the fortune teller's shop so we could verify that it was the pendant that was enabling me to see Rolfe's true nature."

"And?"

"Well, nothing. When I took the pendant off, he went back to looking like the Rolfe I'd met earlier when I thought he was a fortune-teller. I slipped it back on, and I could see the vampire side of him again."

"The real him. There is no other side of a vampire," the driver growled.

I scowled at the back of his head.

"Elsie, I feel witch magic. And it's strong. We located a box in her apartment with the same magical signature." Anton turned toward Cassandra. "Was the pendent held in a small blue box?"

I nodded. Reality was settling back in, and I still had things to take care of. Plus, I was getting hungry and needed to check my blood.

"Hey, I need to go back for my backpack and my car. If you won't let me go to the job site, you've got to at least let me get my blood testing kit and insulin. And I need to call people and make arrangements for my job. It's a government building. People are going to get worried and start looking for me."

"She's right. The Ancient Lake is only a few hours from you. Go forth and perform the awakening ritual to summon her magic. Then head back to Sacramento and let her wrap up as much of her life as she can before bringing her to Thornwood," Elsie instructed.

"Wait, how many hours is a few hours from Sac? Where is this Ancient Lake?" I grabbed the back of the seat and leaned forward as much as my seat belt would allow. "And what exactly is an Ancient Lake anyway?"

"A body of freshwater older than a million years, and lucky us, we have one within driving distance," Blue said

"Whoa." I'd never heard of an ancient lake before and to think there was one so close by.

"Many Naturals live and travel to the Ancient Lake daily, so be careful and watch your surroundings. Cassandra, if you see, feel, or hear anything you must let the wolves know right away. It's their job to handle anything that might stand in your way." Elsie took a deep breath. "Be watchful. We already know there is death magic trying to stop you. Now we know a vampire is aware of Cassandra. This news makes the quest increasingly more dangerous."

"Yes, and is the death magic maker working with the vampire?" Blue asked.

"It would be extremely unusual. Vampire avoid Necromancers, from my experience. But if they did join forces, we would be up against insurmountable odds," Elsie said quietly.

"Yes, but we have witches," Anton shouted and slapped his thigh. "Not just one but two. Those vamps don't stand a chance against us!"

"You have one witch and a human with magic she doesn't know how to use," Elsie hissed over the truck speakers. "You are too young to remember, but the Blood Wars alone almost wiped us off the face of this planet. The witch burnings finished what the Blood Wars couldn't, thanks to the Vampire and their influence over humans. Now is not the time to show your balls, you fool. We must remain cunning and sure in our movements if we have any hope of winning the day."

An eerie silence filled the truck. This didn't sound like something I wanted to be involved in.

"First, I don't think the Vampires know about me. I told Rolfe to forget about me. Second, can't I just give you whatever magic I'm supposed to have?" I asked.

"It doesn't work like that," Blue whispered.

"You are the first of the Thirteen. If we lost one of you, we've lost it all. The weight of our survival falls to each soul that must be awakened. Every one of you needs to come together to complete the coven. Only then will your witch soul awaken and allow you to remember your true self."

"I think you might have the wrong girl." I wiggled in my seat. It was getting hot inside the truck. "I'm pretty sure I know who I am. My true self doesn't want to be a witch that has red-eyed Death Ravens coming for her."

"You don't have a choice. There isn't a switch that turns who you are off. This is your true self, Cassandra. Your magic is coming in because it knows you are in danger and it is time. At least perform the awakening ritual so you have a chance to feel your power. Not that you can go back, because they will still hunt you, regardless if you bring forth your magic or not. They have your scent. They will never leave you alone now. You will always have creatures hunting you simply because you are a witch. Anyone close to you will be in danger. We are still your best ... your only chance to remain alive."

"That's just it. I'm not a witch."

"Oh, you're all witch, honey," Anton barked on a laugh.

I turned toward him and said, "Stop talking."

Anton's smile faded, and he turned forward-facing without saying another word.

"Measure your words, Witch," Elsie said.

I felt her essence move over me right down to the center of my whole being. I wasn't quite sure if she said it in my head or over the phone.

"Reverse your influence, Cassandra," she said in the same manner.

"I take my words back," I watched Anton to see if it worked. I'd not tried to take back something I'd said yet. His eyes moved and the smile he'd had when I'd influenced him spread across his mouth again, my shoulders relaxed. His eyes met mine, and I experienced a pang of guilt over what I'd done to him.

"I'd request you not extend your influence over your wolves until you have a better idea of how to properly use it," Elsie said.

"You didn't have a problem with me," I used my fingers for air quotes, even though she couldn't see them, "'using my influence' to get away from the demon birds."

"Death Ravens," Blue interjected.

I faced him and mouthed, "Seriously?"

"There is a large distinction between using what limited magic you have to save the lot of you from being torn apart by a flock of murderous Death Ravens versus using your influence to shut someone up when you don't like what they've said."

She was right and I knew it. I was being a jerk, but I couldn't seem to stop myself.

I wanted to pretend that none of this was real or I was in the middle of a long dream. I wanted to close my eyes and have everything be back to before the night terror that started it all.

"I won't use my words against you again," I mumbled, and gave Anton a half-smile. "I'm sorry."

"It's okay. Maybe you could influence me to fly or be super strong or something that would help us?" he asked.

"You might want to hold off using undisciplined magic on each other until the awakening ritual has been performed," Elsie said dryly.

"Doesn't change the fact that I still need my testing kit and insulin. I'm going to need to eat soon or it won't matter if the murder birds catch us because I'll be in a diabetic coma."

Thaddeus took the next exit without another word. "Looks like we have hamburgers, tacos or sandwiches available. Which do you prefer?"

"Sandwiches would be best. I can order a few, so I have food along the way."

"You need to eat every couple of hours?" Thaddeus asked, watching me in the rearview mirror.

"I do. I need insulin, and I need to be able to test myself."

"The bag we recovered from her apartment is in the bed of the truck. Maybe there's something salvageable in it."

"There's not," I said sadly. "I watched the insulin break when I fell trying to escape my condo."

"Wish it so, Cassandra," Elsie said over the speaker.

"What?"

"Wish with all your heart that your insulin and testing device are unharmed and functional in your bag."

"But they aren't."

"They aren't because you see that in your mind's eye. Wipe that image away and visualize what you desire. Then push your magic toward it by wishing... wish with all of your heart and soul for your medical items. It's life or death. Yours and ours."

Thaddeus pulled into the popular sandwich shop's parking lot, and the others bailed out of the truck. Anton whipped the door he'd just exited open and deposited my charred black go-bag on the seat next to me. I clenched my fists and squeezed my eyes closed as hard as I could and wished with all my might that my testing kit and all my insulin was in my bag in perfect condition. I'd not tried to manifest anything since finding my new gift. I'd only influenced the things and situations around me. If I could do this, everything would change. I'd never want for anything, and everything I could imagine would be available to me.

After I felt an appropriate amount of wishing had happened, I reached into my bag, not afraid of what I would find or unsure what would be waiting for me. Instead, I reached in and wrapped my fingers around my blood tester and a vile of insulin and pulled them out. I went in with the expectation that they would be there and they were. Then, I visualized a syringe in the safety pocket I kept them in and pulled it out too.

I felt a little giddy at what happened. I kept my excitement to myself, but my inner being was making plans. This changed everything. I could do so much with my new powers. I could bring on world peace, if I concentrated hard enough, cure cancer... or even end famine. The opportunities were endless. I kept all that stuffed deep down, but I'm not going to lie.. it was hard.

Now, instead of being anxious to get back, I was excited to get to this Ancient Lake and see what other magic I'd be able to use to help people.

We ordered food to go. I took care of my testing and insulin shot while the lot of them used the facilities. Thaddeus drilled me on what supplies I needed, what my favorite drinks and foods were, and then finally, we stocked up on water, chips, and extra sandwiches, filled the gas tank, and hit the road.

"Hey, exactly where is this Ancient Lake, anyway?" I asked around a mouthful of my Turkey and Swiss after we'd been back on the road for twenty minutes.

Chapter 16

Declutter your home!

Out with the old, in with the new, winds of change

I welcome you!

"Lake Tahoe!" I yelled as the truck pulled over the mountain

and the thick forest cut away to frame the sparkling body of

water. "Lake Tahoe is an Ancient Lake? That's so cool and

kind of incredible to think I've lived so close to it and didn't

know!"

I was bouncing in my seat. I'd spent the rest of the ride to the

lake, after the realization of what I might be capable of,

thinking about all the possible ways I could improve the

quality of life for everyone. The first thing I wanted to do was

bring back Mr. Miller and Bootsie. Just reverse that whole

situation so that it never happened.

The glistening water seemed to be calling to me. Every time

the truck drove around a bend and the sapphire blue water

was hidden from my view, I grabbed the seat and bounced my feet. I could feel the energy pouring from the giant body of water, and I was addicted.

"I'm embarrassed to say I've never bothered to visit Tahoe," I said, entranced by its beauty. The thick overhead canopy blocked the sun from the road and only served to enhance the deep blue of the lake.

"Which beach are we going to?" I asked.

"We can't go to a human-populated beach. We need to find an area with enough space to do the ritual out of view of human eyes," Thaddeus said from behind the wheel.

"Not just humans. There will be a gathering of Naturals there," Blue said.

"Who are the Naturals?" I asked.

"Naturals are other magical beings." Blue's face was turned away from me. He was watching the forest flash by and seemed to be lost in thought.

"Why are they called Naturals? Why not call them Magicals?" The truck grew quiet, and I could feel something brewing. There was a story here that they didn't want to share with me. Or were uncomfortable sharing, anyway.

"Naturals are natural. They are beings who are a part of nature. Without nature, they die."

"Are you all Naturals?"

"Unbound wolves are Naturals. Once a wolf binds his soul to a witch, he ceases to be classified as a Natural."

"Why? Wouldn't that make him supernatural?"

"Witches aren't Naturals," Anton whispered.

I turned toward him and asked, "What? Why?"

"Naturals require nature for their magic. Witches don't require anything but themselves for their magic. Their magic comes from somewhere else."

"Where?" I was floored to learn this. Did that mean witches were unnatural?

"That's a question for Elsie," Blue said.

"Are witches the only unnatural beings?"

"Witches aren't unnatural. They're probably the most natural beings in existence. They just don't pull magic from nature. They don't have to," Blue replied.

"This doesn't make sense." I couldn't be the only one confused. I looked at Anton. "Does this make sense to you?"

He shrugged his shoulders, and I realized he may not know the answers to some of this stuff either.

"Witches are magical all by themselves. They don't need to pull magic from anywhere. They already have it within. Other magical creatures are part of nature and need to be in nature to survive or they lose their magic and die. Which is why the magical world hates humans."

My head whipped toward Blue. "Hates humans? What did humans do?"

"Humans kill nature. They go against nature at every turn. Humans are the only truly unnatural beings on the planet."

"Except Vamps," Roan muttered from the front seat.

"What about Vampires?" I asked.

"Vampires are humans who were infected by the Vamp virus before they died. Except now they live off of the blood of humans. So for them the more humans, the better. It's their only food source."

I sat back. Rolfe didn't seem like he thought of me as a food source. Although he did say he was going to sell me, so he didn't see me as an equal either. Humans were unnatural? I guess that made sense but also seemed wrong.

"So, who's attacking us?" I asked.

"Death Magic, not a who, but a what." Roan turned in his seat to pin me with a hard look.

"What does that mean?"

"The beings after us want to wipe out humanity so nature can flourish again. The only way to do that is to eliminate the Last Witch and ensure the Thirteen never awaken."

"What do the witches have to do with humanity?"

Silence fell over the truck. "That's another question for Elsie." Roan turned back toward the front of the truck. Guess that conversation was done.

Goosebumps covered my arms as Thaddeus pulled the truck off the highway and down a narrow dirt road. Well, I guess you could call it a road. It resembled more of a path. Branches scraped along the truck like nails on a chalkboard. I knew the paint was trashed, but no one in the cab of the truck seemed to mind but me.

Thaddeus pulled the vehicle to a stop, and all four doors swung open at once.

My excitement outweighed my apprehension, and I quickly followed the men to the edge of the lake at a small clearing. Anton and Thaddeus broke off a large branch and went to work clearing and marking the ground. I was mesmerized by the brilliant blue water and walked towards its edge.

The water sparkled like a million cut diamonds. It was the most beautiful thing I'd seen in real life. Lake Tahoe was stunning in photos, but they couldn't truly capture the intensity of the vast, deep blue water. Absentmindedly, I leaned over and traced a line with a swish and a squiggly line across it in the soft dirt.

I exhaled the breath I didn't realize I'd been holding, and hadn't noticed I'd gotten so close when a thick slimy hand reached up from the water and grabbed my ankle.

I screamed, of course, because one, it was gross and slimy, and two, it was trying to pull me into the water. And while I had a feeling the water would somehow fuel me; I didn't think being hauled under by whatever was on the other end of the slimy hand would be helpful to me in any way.

I screamed again when it tugged so hard, I landed on my rear as I was being dragged to the water's edge.

Luckily, the guys rushed to my side.

Thaddeus reached me first and wrapped himself around my torso. "If it pulls you in, I'll stay with you," he growled, and I saw that his eyes had turned amber.

I'm not going to lie. I clung to him.

I didn't want to go any further into the water, but if it did yank me all the way in, I really didn't want to go in alone. I know it was selfish, and I had a fleeting moment of shame, but not enough to let go of him as my lifeline.

The others arrived as well and fought to keep the large gross hand from pulling me under. We were losing the fight because it managed to get my other leg in the water, and I panicked. I intensified my flailing about. It didn't matter how hard I fought or what the guys did, it wouldn't let go, and now my entire lower body was below the surface.

I clung to Thaddeus with everything in me, as Anton and Blue dove into the water to battle whatever kind of creature was attacking us now.

We watched as the surface swished about, and bubbles exploded just below the surface. I couldn't see what was happening under the water, but the struggle seemed to be intensifying when the grip it had on my ankle tightened painfully.

"They've been under too long," Roan yelled and dove in.

"I think it's crushing my bones," I gasped.

"Tell it to let you go," Thaddeus said in my ear. "Now Cassandra, tell it now."

The pain was unbearable and half of me wanted to go into the water with it just to make it stop.

"Let me go!" I screamed and pushed as much of myself into that command as I could. The headache that had receded during the ride to the lake, came rushing back and brought its friend nausea along for the ride.

The grip on my ankle ceased immediately, and Thaddeus pulled me back with such force, I landed on top of him. We watched in horror as blood floated to the top of the now still surface.

"No!" I screamed. "Bring them back!" I closed my eyes and through the pain, I pictured the three men who'd risked their lives for mine. I saw them healthy, breaking through the water and swimming to shore.

I opened my eyes to watch that exact thing happen, identical to what I'd pictured. I was so relieved to see them I tried to stand but collapsed from the worst agony I'd ever felt in my life. The men broke free of the surface and ran to me at once.

"Get her to the circle. She doesn't have to be standing," Thaddeus yelled, and they moved me to the center of the marks Anton had made in the dirt.

Blue placed something that stunk to high heaven around my neck, a crystal in my hand, and a rolled parchment paper in my other hand, and moved back.

"Everyone in place?" he asked.

Once he received "Yeah" all around, he said to me, "Cassandra, read the parchment. Read it now!" I looked to the lake, and the surface of the water began splashing and bubbling on its own.

"Read it now before it surfaces!" he yelled.

I tore my eyes from whatever was going to bust through the lake and looked at the parchment in my hand.

"*So so simi delica ono barifia blismals aliicia,*" I read. I could feel something happening. My body felt like an electrical current was building up inside, and when it reached its full level, I would somehow be recharged. I braced for it to run through me.

"Read it again!" Blue yelled. The lake was frothing and bubbling, and whatever was coming up was big. As in, huge. I looked back down to the parchment and read the words again. I didn't understand with my brain what they meant, but my body and soul understood completely.

I felt white-hot energy rushing through me. My muscles ached, and my bones grew weary. My vision went blurry and out of focus and then snapped back sharp and clear.

Something shivered across my skin, and I knew it was my magic finding its place. Settling in. Something inside my chest exploded and threw me back.

I heard Blue warn the men to stay where they were.

My fingers began tingling again as they did after my night terror. The pain in my ankle intensified and then in a snap completely went away. Something was building up inside of me, and it felt like it was clawing to escape. It hurt like heck, and I wanted to give it a way out so I opened my mouth.

"Who dared an attempt to stop my awakening?" I roared in a voice I've never heard, much less used before. I could feel every vein, muscle, and bone in my body. Weird things were happening, my blood was running backward. How did I know? No idea, but I knew something was inside of me taking inventory... stock of what I was.

The newly awakened side of me was busy; anything it found lacking was examined and repaired. And it was happening at the speed of light, whether I wanted it to or not. I'd never felt this aware, or this connected to my body before, ever.

The throbbing in my head lightened bit by bit until the torture was wiped completely away.

Thinking back, I don't know how long I withered around on the ground, but I know it stopped the second the lake monster broke clear of the surface. My body seemed to know what it wanted and that was to meet the monster head-on. I only had a brief moment to see it and take in its enormous size before it attacked.

It had a dome-shaped head and big bug eyes. Its skin was slimy and a grayish-green and stunk to high heaven. Its mouth opened to screech and showed row upon row of sharp, jagged, uneven teeth. Mesmerized, I watched as it brought one of its hands out of the water and placed it onshore as if to pull itself out of the lake.

Around me, the men were thrashing about too, but only for a moment. I watched transfixed as they shifted into wolves and lunged for the monster in unison. Now I understood why they referred to themselves as wolves. They were larger than any wolf I'd ever seen on TV. Big, strong, and deadly. Easily twice my size, they were immense.

I watched as a lone wolf pulled away and launched itself at one of the monster's eyes. It must have done some damage because the monster screeched again and smacked the wolf away. As big and powerful as the wolves were, they were no match for the size of the monster that now placed its second hand on the shore. I watched in horror as I grasped that it was going to make it out of the water!

One of the wolves cried out in pain as it landed a few feet from me. I held my breath for what seemed like a century, waiting to see if he would get back up. I released it when he tried, only to fall back to his side. I pulled myself up, and ran to him as fast as I could. I laid my hands on his black wet body.

"Heal yourself, wolf." My fingers tingled.

The words came from my mouth, but it was not my voice. Warmth spread from my palms to his body, and I could feel his ligaments mending and his shattered bones snapping back into place. He was panting hard, and I knew he was in severe pain. Another wolf landed a few feet from me, and I watched as yet another tried to pull himself out of the water only to fall back in. Which one was that? Who was in the water? I panicked and looked at the monster.

We were losing. These men, wolves, had risked their lives for mine, and we were losing.

We had to get out of there before we all died. I straightened my body to its full height.

"Creature of the lake, go back to where you came from and never pursue us again!" I screamed and thrust my hands at it. Blue and Green sparks flew from my fingers. My blood warmed as it rushed through my veins, and my head pounded. I collapsed to the ground, panting... watching... praying.

And just like that, as soon as my words were spoken, the monster immediately sank back into the water on a gurgling screech. Clearly, it wasn't happy it had to obey my wishes. Without waiting to see what else might happen, I ran to the wolf who had landed next to me. While I did that, Blue transformed back into a naked man and dove into the water. I watched him pull one of the other wolves to shore.

With tingling fingers and a pounding head, I laid my hands on the wet red fur and said, "Heal yourself, Wolf."

I felt the same as before as the bones and muscles moved and repaired themselves as they had with Blue the first time.

"Cassandra," Blue shouted as he laid a brown wolf on the shore only to dive back into the water.

I ran to the still wolf but as I neared, I slowed my pace. I didn't feel life coming from him and something about that made me feel feral. My vision took on a red haze and anger like I've never felt before flooded my system. I dropped to my knees and did the same as the other two, but nothing happened. He didn't heal or whimper or move in any way. Blue broke free of the surface with the other brown wolf and hefted the large animal ashore.

I ran to that wolf and laid my hands on him.

"Heal yourself, Wolf," I cried, desperate for him to live. The second Blue was clear of him, he cried out from the pain of his muscles and bones mending back into place as they should be. I was so relieved, I sobbed out loud, tears streaming down my face. Without a word, I turned on my heel and moved back to the unmoving brown wolf who I couldn't heal earlier.

"He's gone, Cassandra," Roan said next to me.

I looked back and saw Blue and Anton naked as the day they were born walking toward us and looked back down at Thaddeus' broken wolf body. He was so beautiful. His fur was soft and thick. I snuggled into his limp form. I wrapped my body around him just as he had wrapped his body around mine to keep the monster from dragging me into the lake.

I buried my face into his neck, and with all the power I could feel strumming through my body whispered, "You live. I demand it. Get up, shake it off, and pledge yourself to me so we can get back on the road and away from here."

The wolf I'd been whispering to trembled, and I loosened my hold, then he shivered, and I relaxed my arms. When he finally stiffened, relief washed over me.

The four of us watched as he popped up on all fours and shook out his fur. The other three men stopped moving abruptly and watched as I stroked his fur with tears streaming down my face, "Thaddeus, I would like you to be my guardian, if you'll have me?" I wrapped my arms around him and kissed his muzzle. I needed to be able to keep an eye on him.

I'd never felt so relieved, sick to my stomach, or thankful as I did at that moment. I would never let anyone die because of me. Ever.

The three other wolves threw their heads back and howled to the sky as Thaddeus transformed from wet wolf to wet naked man while my hand rested on his head.

"At your command, Witch," he said in a low growl.

Chapter 17

Kindness is never wrong.

The stench of death and decay permeated the skeleton-

lined cavern. A continuous drip sounded somewhere in one of

the many tunnels that shot out from the cavern. Centuries in

the large cave meant many tunnels had been dug to no avail.

The Oracle moved around in its chamber, dragging the heavy

chain that had burdened its leg for so long, the pain and

discomfort it caused no longer mattered.

The days had turned into weeks and months until years

became decades, and now that several centuries had gone by,

the world above would no longer recognize the Oracle's kind.

The Oracle shivered and shook as much as her old body

would allow as she stepped out of her leathery skin. With this

cycle's ecdysis complete, the oracle sighed, the ripping away

of the discarded skin around where the chain was connected

would be painful and painstaking.

A slimy serpent appeared from where it was hiding in the shadow among the bones.

"Master wishes the hide," it said.

"The Master can wait until I'm done shedding it, can't he?" the Oracle snarled at the serpent. "Or would he prefer you rip it from my body?"

The serpent's eyes glowed red. "He desires it now."

The Oracle shuffled away from her discarded scales and allowed the recesses of the cavern to swallow her from sight. The serpent waited a beat and watched the shadows where he saw the Oracle disappear. He was never sure if the giant beast left completely or if she watched and waited. The serpent slithered to the hide to retrieve it, and the Oracle reappeared.

"I'll be sure to thank the Master for the morsel," the Oracle said. It was the last thing the serpent heard before the Oracle bared her deadly fangs and bit the head of the serpent off. Usually, the Oracle would eat two or three of the servants sent to retrieve her discarded hide. Only when its belly was full would she relinquish it.

It was a game they played. Her and the insidious Master who held her captive.

In the beginning, there was a smidge of hope of escape. As the years dragged on and the Master became weary of experimenting on the Oracle, hopes of rescue kept her from falling into the recesses of despair.

After that came the first vision that changed everything. The one that showed the Oracle what had happened to her kind over the centuries of being held deep below the earth in the death chambers, their fate and many other creatures, as they were wiped from the world they knew. So many lost. So many never to walk the earth again.

She swallowed the head and tore apart the rest of the body with her talons before devouring all of it. The Oracle was on a mission to regain her strength. The wings may have been stolen from her back, but the Oracle was the last of her kind, and her kind was deadly.

She'd seen the end and knew the only hope for her vengeance laid with the Thornwood witches. Specifically, the Last Witch. She'd only seen glimpses; the visions were still unclear what role she was to play, and the outcome was grainy. But the vision was clear about one thing. The battle between the witches and the Master was at hand, and the winner would determine life on Earth for all the creatures who called it home. The Oracle cared little about that. Her only focus was seeking vengeance by destroying the Master.

She needed to figure out a way to trick the Master into bringing one of the Thirteen to her. It was the only way to lure the Last Witch there and destroy the Master. He was powerful but still no match for her, the Last Witch.

Without her, the vision was incomplete.

A thud roused her from her musings. The Oracle didn't bother to look up. She could smell the vile creature before it reached her. She continued to lick her talons and prepared for her next morsel of tribute before she'd allow the Master to have her hide.

Dark Magic was all the hide could be used for. No good could come from it. The Master didn't have the skills required to utilize the tough hide's properties. That meant he was trading or bargaining with Dark Magic makers.

Desolate times ahead. The best she could hope for was a quick death. Something the Master promised over and over, only to find the loophole that allowed him to betray the original bargain. A deal she'd made to save his clan. An agreement that unknowingly sealed the deadly fate of her kind forever. The Oracle was banking that the Last Witch would provide the death she craved for so many centuries. She only needed to get her to this chamber for the vision to become reality.

Chapter 18

Natural witches will often find themselves in the company of animals, by preference.

Once I was sure the wolves were going to live and had no injuries that needed my immediate attention, I snuck away for some privacy. I lowered myself to the ground next to a large, fallen tree. The battle we'd just fought had shaken me to my core, my head pounded and I was sick to my stomach. But also, I now had vast amounts of powerful magic running through my body... and it felt right. Somehow, I knew what I was capable of and I wanted nothing more than to use it. All of it.

Today, I'd done what I'd been created to do and was finally able to use my magic in a manner that had always been frowned upon before. How did I know this? I didn't have a clue. It was ingrained in me. Deep in my soul, I knew I was there to fix, heal, and repair. Something others were afraid of.

It was a part of myself I'd need to guard and protect. Others would try to shut my power down.

Thinking of the wolves who'd fought so hard for me brought on a smile. A big one.

Because I knew I'd done something miraculous. I'd wished them all back from death. First, when the lake filled with their blood, then when they'd lost Thaddeus. They'd all been gone. I was in tune with them and felt their life force leaving their bodies each time. I didn't even have to think about it; it was natural and right for me to save them. Bring them all back. There was a dark memory I couldn't quite grab hold of but knew was important. Something I needed to remember but it was just out of my grasp. Maybe an old memory, from the soul I carried within me.

I had it now. I knew how to use my magic to help instead of only in reaction mode. I closed my eyes through the pain in my head I wished for my black backpack. Since I could visualize it, I felt pretty strongly that I could bring it to me. It had worked with the insulin, so why couldn't it work with other things? I pictured it on my back and remembered the feel of the weight of it and how the straps pressed gently across my shoulders.

"My backpack is on my back where it belongs," I said out loud and knew the second the last word had left my mouth the backpack was with me. Relief flooded my entire body. I laughed and whipped it around to the front.

Next up, I closed my eyes and thought about the condo and how it was before the attack. I pictured the newlyweds upstairs on Saturday morning with their windows open and their music blasting for the neighborhood to get mad about. I saw Old Man Miller walking Bootsie on her leash in my mind's eye and said, "Make the condo and its inhabitants exactly as they were before the attack." And vomited the sandwiches that we'd eaten earlier. Was I getting sick? Or was my blood sugar off?

I sat very still for a few moments, calmed my empty stomach while visualizing my condo and its inhabitants. Once I felt good about the image in my mind, I dug around in my bag for my cell phone. Relief washed over me when my hand wrapped around it and I pulled it out. I wished one last time as an extra measure, "Please let them all be okay." Looking down at my screen I found Old Man Miller's contact and touched it.

And held my breath.

"Hello," he answered after only one ring.

I broke out in a full-body flush, tears fell, and I gripped the phone. I worked to disguise my emotions, "Mr. Miller? It's Cassandra."

"Well, top of the mornin' to ya. What can I do ya for?" He always was such a dork. I smiled to myself again as the tears continued to fall.

"I wanted to let you know I had to move out of town in an emergency but not to worry. I'll be sending someone soon to clean the condo out."

I looked at my feet and realized this may very well be the last time I would speak to my friend. He would be in serious danger if I ever had anything to do with him. For that matter, anyone who wasn't prepared to fight for their lives at a moment's notice would be in grave danger around me.

"Mr. Miller, thank you for all you've done for me. I'll miss you."

"Oh no, that's just terrible news. It just won't be the same around here without you, Cassie. Who will I spend the holidays with?"

I heard the disappointment in his voice and couldn't stand it. It made me do something impulsive, and out of sheer selfishness because I couldn't stand him being lonely.

I pushed as much power into my voice as I could. I wasn't sure if this thing would work over the phone.

"Mr. Miller, you won't miss me at all. In fact, you've forgotten me, for the most part. You'll only think of me fondly once in a while. You'll start walking with Mrs. Abernathy, and both of you will fall head over heels in love, and you'll live happily ever after." The headache I'd been nursing rushed back front and center with a vengeance.

The line was silent, and I didn't know if it worked. If it didn't, he was going to think I'd had some kind of mental meltdown. "Mr. Miller?"

"Yes, who's there?"

Chills ran over my skin and I massaged my temple.

"Sorry, wrong number," I whispered and disconnected the call.

Well, I knew I should feel good that it worked remotely, but somehow it left me feeling morose. The next call I made was to my quasi partner, Dawn. I power-talked her into finishing the project, creating the invoice, and told her how to make sure the payment was digitally deposited into my business account. That call did leave me feeling better. I was happy I'd saved it for last.

Then I remembered that I'd need to deal with my condo. Whether I stayed with the wolves or moved somewhere else, it would have to be somewhere without neighbors who might be fire bombed while they slept.

I sat on the log in complete stillness and allowed myself to have a few moments to mourn my past life.

Self-care was still a thing.

***

"I was dead," Thaddeus whispered to Alicaster Blue, and then pulled his shirt over his head.

"Not fully. You couldn't have been," Blue replied.

"I'm telling you I was gone. Heading to the other side, when I heard her command me back. I had no choice." Thaddeus slipped his feet into his shoes.

Alicaster Blue halted pulling on his boots and looked at his friend. "Keep it to yourself until we reach the Last Witch and then tell her, if you must tell anyone. Death Magic is strictly forbidden. She's too new and doesn't know her powers or the rules yet."

"I'm not complaining. I'm glad she brought me back. And I don't think what she did was the same as necromancy. I have no desire to eat your flesh."

"Good thing. Be a cryin' shame to put all her hard work to waste by killing you again."

The men stopped talking when Anton moved closer.

"Okay, listen up. We need to get back on the road and to Cassandra's car so she can retrieve her bag ..." Anton said before Cassandra interrupted him as she broke through the forest edge.

"You mean this bag?" she asked, stepping out from the dense trees holding up a backpack.

"Where did that come from?" Anton asked.

"I believed I had it, and here it is." She smiled and held up her backpack higher.

The Wolves looked at each other and shared an uncomfortable silence.

"Does this mean we can go straight to Thornwood?" Roan asked, breaking the weird vibe that had seeped into their proximity.

Cassandra held up her phone. "I already called and told them my friend Dawn would be finishing up for me and made payment arrangements. It's all handled."

The Wolves watched her before Roan said, "Let's get on the road. It'll be dark in a couple of hours, and I'd like to be as close to our coast and mountains as possible. It's not safe here."

They busied themselves packing back into the truck and backtracking out of the dense forest the way they had come into it.

"Could you spell us to Thornwood?" Anton asked, once they were on the highway.

"I don't think that's a good idea," Blue grumbled, and caught Thaddeus' eye in the rearview mirror.

"I couldn't anyway. So far, I am only able to work things I can see in my mind. A memory, or proximity, are big factors for me."

"Do you feel any different?" Blue asked.

"I feel sick to my stomach and my head still hurts. That part didn't change... otherwise, I feel strong, alert, powerful. It's hard to explain. Like this other side of me has been asleep my whole life and now is awake and it's a really good side!"

Blue studied her as she looked out the window.

"Colors are more intense. I can smell everything in the air. I can hear your heartbeats. Smell your bodies." She smiled.

"Not just smell, but feel your life force. Like, I could command you to stop breathing if I wanted to, or your heart to stop beating."

The wolves had her full attention.

"I wouldn't! I would never hurt any of you!"

"The sooner we get back to Thornwood, the better," Roan grumbled.

"Can you hear our thoughts?" Blue asked.

"No..."

He watched her eyes flash to the driver's seat.

"You don't sound a hundred percent sure."

"Well, there is one thing....no, I can't hear anyone's thoughts. It's more like I'm in tune with your life force. It's like I can sense you're alive, maybe? I can't explain it. I can see the life moving in the trees, the animals, us. I'm a part of it now."

He watched her eyes flash again and knew there was more to it. Alicaster Blue would be reporting everything he'd experienced so far to Max and Elsie. They would know how to handle the new witch and help her with her powers.

The rest of the trip was mostly spent in silence from the wolves. Periodically, Thaddeus would ask her if she needed to eat or use the facilities.

Eventually. After he asked her for the eleventy-thousandth time, she said, "Thaddeus, I know you're trying to take care of me, so how about I let you know if I need to stop?"

He watched her from the rearview mirror and grunted.

Cassandra synced her device to the truck's sound system, and they were forced to endure her playlist full of songs about heartbreak and redemption. Mostly by female artists. Alicaster Blue mused that even though he'd listened to the song three times, he still had no idea what a hollaback girl was.

The low sun filtered through the dense forest as the truck turned off of the two-lane highway onto a meandering drive toward Thornwood. After several hours of being cramped up in the truck, Cassandra watched the Pacific Ocean as the cobblestone road wound atop the jagged cliff overlooking the white crested waves as they crashed against the jutting stone.

"This is so pretty," she gasped. "Can we stop and look for a minute?"

"We can't stop until we make it onto Thornwood's grounds and its protection. There will be plenty of time to explore once you're safe," Thaddeus answered.

"Yeah, that, and Max would skin us alive if we made a pit stop so close to arriving." Anton laughed. "Aren't you excited to meet her? She's one of the most powerful beings on earth...."

Cassandra spotted a lone figure at the edge of the forest. He was dressed in some kind of crude medieval black armor and was holding a spear. His entire being seemed devoid of light. Like he was a black hole where all bright and shiny objects went to die.

She blinked, and he was gone. The truck skidded around another bend, and the same soldier appeared on the opposite side of the vehicle, this time at the edge of the cliff.

His red glowing eyes were intent on her. He could see her, and she could see him. A shiver of dark times ahead skimmed over her as they locked gazes.

"Tell me you guys see that soldier," she said.

"Where?" Thaddeus barked.

She pointed to where he'd been standing but was now gone.

"He was just there, but that was the second time I'd seen him. The first time he was near the forest."

"What did he look like?" Thaddeus asked.

"Black, the blackest black I'd ever seen with old-time armor and a spear. Oh, and red glowing eyes."

Thaddeus stepped on the gas just as the same black soldier appeared in front of the truck. This time it bared large deadly fangs and snarled at her. A warning. Her skin felt the same shiver as before.

"There," she screamed and pointed straight ahead as they barreled through what she now realized must have been a specter. As the truck passed through the aberration a bone-chilling cold washed over Cassandra.

"I saw nothing," Thaddeus said.

"Me either," Anton said, and the other two agreed.

"D-did you f-feel the c-cold?" She chattered.

The Wolves howled at once. "Go, Thaddeus! Step on it!" Alicaster Blue yelled. "We need to get her to Thornwood before he strikes!"

"You'll be safer there. You're the only being on earth like her," Blue said, searching the woods. "At least until more of your coven are awoken."

"I'm the first of thirteen witches. What happens when we are all awake?"

"That's a question for Elsie," Blue mumbled.

The truck made a sharp right turn away from the cliff edge and into the thick forest. Cassandra grabbed the back of the seats in front of her to brace as they bounced around inside the cab. She held her breath as long as she could, the truck was literally driving through the forest. No road, no trail, no path, just forest floor, and squeezing through close trees and occasionally avoiding logs.

They drove for what seemed to Cassandra an hour, but in reality, it was only twenty minutes before they pulled onto the edge of a vast mustard field and stopped.

The wolves swung the doors open and exited the vehicle with Cassandra close behind.

"Do you see him, Casandra?" Thaddeus asked, and hurried to help her from the truck.

"No." She looked around with Thaddeus at her side. "I don't see him anywhere."

"Stay at my back, no matter what happens," Thaddeus growled and moved her to safety behind him.

Cassandra grabbed fistfuls of the back of his shirt and held on.

"We may be too close to Thornwood for it to comfortably travel."

"Now where do we go?" The group stood at the edge of the meadow feeling exposed.

"We wait. Now, we wait." Blue stood on the other side of Cassandra with his arms crossed. None of them liked being out in the open.

Cassandra looked around at her new friends and decided to mimic their stance.

"A unified front. How touching," a woman drawled from behind them.

Cassandra screamed, and two of the wolves dropped to a crouch. Blue looked at Thaddeus over Anton's and Roan's heads and smirked. They were the only two left standing.

Once she recovered from being scared nearly to death, Cassandra recognized the woman immediately. The white braids, clusters of charms and crystals hanging from around her neck, and face tattoos were a dead giveaway. A large gorgeous man, whom Cassandra assumed must also be a Wolf, remained at her back. He towered over her and mirrored her movements from behind.

"Hi," Cassandra said tentatively and her wolves closed in around her.

"Protective, too, I see. Well, this is much better than we could have hoped for." The Last Witch approached the group and took Cassandra by her elbow, looping her arm through. "Let's show you your new home, shall we? We have a lot of work to do before your sisters arrive."

"Sisters?"

Chapter 19

Words have power, use them wisely.

"**C**oven sisters." the Last Witch finally spoke. "Soon it'll be
time to wake the others up. We don't have as much time as
I'd hoped for. I'm afraid it's going to be a race against the
clock for each of them."

Elsie, the Last Witch, chatted me up the whole walk to her
beautiful home. Which was so much more than a home and a
bit more like an estate. Or a prepper's dream compound. At a
glance, the property had several large ponds, a couple of
streams, stables, a corral, a few barns, more gardens than I
could count, and several buildings scattered along the path
that led to one of the largest homes I'd ever seen in person...
and I've worked in some seriously large homes.

It was a kind of a mashup of Victorian, Gothic and Tudor
styles. The roof showcased several towers with gorgeous
stained glass arched windows and thick black iron weather

vanes that ran along every rooftop. The peaks and turrets were finished in copper and a heavy slate shingle.

Dark carved wood trimmed the doors, windows, and corners of the vast home. The walls were a soft silvery sage, and plants were growing everywhere. Blue pots in various shapes and sizes over-flowed with lush plants of more varieties than I could count.

I noted no less than five chimneys from the front and a wide porch that spanned the entire face of the home on both sides. I'd never actually seen a true wraparound porch in real life before. Living in California, the style wasn't prevalent, at least where I'd spent my adulthood.

On the walk to the house, my headache receded and my stomach settled. I relaxed, maybe this was somewhere I could finally find some peace.

The walkway was made up of the same slate as the roof, steps, and porch. A beautiful brilliant blue flower bloomed near the path and I leaned over to smell it when I felt a tug on my arm.

"Don't want to sniff that one, dear. Unless you fancy becoming a new version of yourself." The large dark wolf warned. "I'm Max, stick close and we might keep you walking upright."

I pulled back quickly and looked at Elsie. She was small and lithe. I was fascinated by her thick white braids she'd pulled up and piled on top of her head. Charms and crystals were woven throughout the braid chaos and sparkled in the sunlight like a magnificent misshapen crown. She carried herself as if she were the queen of the world with a quiet confidence, I'd give anything to master.

Her face now was clear of the Nordic style tattoos I'd seen earlier in her hologram projection. Black thick lashes and eyebrows surrounded large almond-shaped silver eyes. She was dressed in a pair of loose blue capris and a long tank top.

A group of incredibly good-looking men rushed forward to meet the guys who were traveling with me. It was hard to tear my eyes away from the loud and outwardly affectionate greeting they received, including rounds of loud back slaps, laughter, and man hugs.

"It's their way," Elsie leaned close to me. "They are loud and smelly, but oh so easy on the eyes." She smiled. "Come on. There is so much to discuss, and we have much to learn about each other. I'd like to start by identifying which soul you have inside of you."

I stopped walking. "Are you going to try to remove it?"

She stopped and looked back at me. "Of course not. It would destroy you both."

"Oh," I said, and moved to follow her into the house as she held the giant door open for me.

When I entered her foyer, it was like coming home. The smells, the filtered daylight, the beautiful dual staircase that curved up both sides of the grand entrance was somehow familiar.

"Have I been here before?" I asked.

Elsie stopped next to me and stood still while watching my reaction.

"No, your original self had not visited this house. But all of my homes have been similar." She shrugged her shoulders. "When you find a style you like, you tend to stick with it."

"I've never felt so at home before." I took in the interior. "I know the kitchen is that way." I pointed to the right hallway under the right stair. "And there's a restroom hidden away under the left stair."

"It's only a water closet."

"Excuse me?" I asked.

"It's not a full bathroom. It's only the toilet and sink. It's for visitors. I've never used it," she replied. "You can slip your shoes off and place them in the cupboard by the door."

"We aren't allowed to wear shoes in the house?"

"It's bad luck."

I tilted my head and studied this small woman who was supposed to be one of the most powerful people on earth as she toed her shoes off and placed them in the cupboard tucked under the stairs.

"You're superstitious?" I asked.

"There is power in superstitions. Each one came about for a reason. The reason we take our shoes off is because they track all sorts of nasty little critters on their bottoms. We don't want to bring them into the home. Back in the dark ages, it was unlucky because the children would get sick and die. Now, it's mostly to show respect for those old traditions. Try not to disregard them so quickly. It's good to be clean. Keep your potions and spells pure by following simple rules of manners. One wrong speck of dirt and your spell to heal a broken branch might cause the tree to grow a lizard's tail. You've no idea how cruel the wood fairies can be when magic mistakes are made. They'd never let you live it down. Trust me, I know." She rolled her eyes.

Talk about being put in my place. I kept quiet and removed my shoes. The cool floor felt wonderful, pretty quickly I felt more relaxed.

"There we go. Now, we have a lot of catching up to do, but first, we need to figure out who you are, don't we?"

I nodded my head in agreement, but honestly, I already knew who I was. I was happier than I'd ever been and felt stronger than I had ever felt, but other than those awesome side effects, everything with me was the same.

In fact, that reminded me. "I need to check my blood sugar. Do you mind if I slip into the restroom?"

I didn't usually hide to test, most people didn't pay attention, and I was quick and discreet, as I'd done it most of my life, but for some reason, I felt out of sorts telling this powerful woman I was weak in any area.

I felt her eyes on me and knew she was working something out. I wasn't brave enough to ask what that thing might be so I studied my toes and decided I needed a pedicure.

"Red would be a good color."

I looked up and met her eyes and realized she knew what I was thinking.

"It's not hard. You're fairly transparent, Cassandra."

Elsie led me toward the left staircase, and I wondered if she forgot I needed to test. "You can test in the Sanctuary. I won't have you hide away. No one will shame you here."

It seemed profound to hear her say those words to me.

"You were the voice in my head telling me to run when I was attacked at the condo." It wasn't a question but a statement. I knew, whether she admitted to it or not.

"Indeed."

Well, so much for her denying it.

"Thank you. You may have saved my life."

"I did save your life. You'd have melted away in the toxic flame like the humans who lived in your building did if you hadn't run when I told you to."

"Shouted."

"Excuse me?"

"You shouted in my head to run. If you'd only told me, I could have ignored you."

"Well," she patted my arm, "you're safe now. I'm sorry for the loss of your friends."

"No loss. They're back to living out their lives as if nothing ever happened thanks to my newfound gifts." I beamed at her. I was pretty proud of my abilities and how I'd used them. I couldn't wait to see what I could learn so I could do more.

"What did you do?" Elsie hissed.

At a glance, I saw that she looked paler than she did a few moments earlier.

"I just wished them back before the attack. I could see it all in my mind. Mr. Miller, Bootsie, and the couple that lived above him. I was very careful to only picture them and not affect anyone else around them. Once I got my backpack and phone back, I called to make sure and just like I'd wished. Mr. Miller was fine." I smiled big and waited for the 'atta girl' I surely deserved.

Instead, Elsie took off running. She sprinted to the stairs and charged them quickly. She was so animated, I giggled and felt compelled to follow her up the wide staircase and through the long hallway, with me hot on her heels. Whatever this tiny woman was running toward or away from, I wanted to be in on it and not left out in the cold. The days of me being the outsider were over, I hoped.

She finally reached her destination and stopped at a pair of tall double doors located at the end of the hallway. She threw both doors open with a swoosh of her hands and rushed inside.

The room was straight out of my favorite fantasy novel, with unbelievably tall ceilings that curved together at a point easily thirty feet above. It had a giant six-panel bay window, wood-paneled walls lined with old maps hanging on them, and shelf after shelf of large leather-bound books of different sizes, and colors.

A large round table stood in the center of the room with an odd-shaped thick map spread across it. Another slightly smaller round table was positioned in the tall bay window area that was three steps lower than the floor in the center of the room. A giant crystal ball rested in the middle of the table and was surrounded by several other smaller orbs of different colors and sizes. The back area sat two steps higher than the center of the room. It housed more shelves full of books and featured a podium made of dark wood. On the podium sat a large opened book that appeared to glow slightly.

The book drew me in, and I turned toward it as Elsie rushed forward in the direction of the bay window. She was quick for her small stature. I climbed the steps and stopped in front of the impressive tome. It was handwritten and had illustrations and what appeared to be dried flowers inside the pages. This was a real-life magic book! I took a deep breath in and reached to turn the page...

"Don't even think about touching that!" she shrieked from across the room.

I snatched my hand back and studied the pages the book was opened to. A screech from the bay window where Elsie was moving around her balls startled me and drew my attention. I went to where she was seated in front of the crystal ball in the center of the table. The thing seemed to be glowing. I know I shouldn't have been surprised after everything I'd been through, but I was.

As I approached, I observed her move the smaller pink and blue spheres around on the table. Under closer inspection, I could see that at the top of the table there was an inlaid silver circle and inside the circle were various silver runes inlaid into the wood as well.

I focused on the crystal ball and saw it was indeed glowing, and a movie had begun playing inside it.

"Cool," I whispered absentmindedly

It looked like the fire at my condo building but in reverse. I watched in horrified wonder as the images included me and Rolfe at Mr. Miller's door, and then continued on as it went further back to before the attack, and then stopped. The crystal ball faded to a pale glowing blue.

Her head swung to me and hissed, "What have you done, Witch?"

I shrugged, "Wasn't that big of a deal..."

"Elsie!" Max charged into the room with Thaddeus who immediately moved across the space to my side. "Tell her what you told me, Wolf."

Thaddeus took my hands and whispered, "I'm so sorry."

I gave him big eyes.

"For what?" I mumbled from the side of my mouth.

"Tell me."

Elsie gave me a hard look, and I knew at that moment, I'd better stay quiet. I'd find out soon enough what the new issue at hand was, even before I found out what the previous issue at hand was. Thaddeus put an arm around me in a show of solidarity.

It didn't make me feel better. In fact, it only served to amp up my nervousness.

"I want to begin by saying I'm happy she did it, and I have zero desire to eat anyone here." Thaddeus squeezed my hand and went on to say, "I was killed by the Monster of the Ancient Lake." Thaddeus let go of my hand and shoved his hand in his pocket.

The Last Witch sat back in her chair. "Go on." She blinked slowly; her silver eyes intense.

"I was gone and heading to the other side," he looked at me, "when I heard her command me back. Next thing I know, I'm awake at the edge of the lake and felt fine. Better than fine. And had zero desire to eat anyone."

I looked at him sideways and mumbled, "Why do you keep saying that?"

Elsie's eyes moved to me for confirmation, and I nodded that what he was reporting was the truth. I wasn't sure what the problem was so I remained quiet.

"You performed Death Magic," Elsie said through gritted teeth.

Chapter 20

When heading into a difficult situation, hang a piece of onyx

around your neck for calmness.

"No, I didn't."

"You brought him back! You brought them all back!" she screeched at me.

"Was I supposed to let him die?" I asked.

"It's not your choice, Cassandra. You must not use your magic to change other people's destinies. Ever." Elsie stood and put her hands on her hips. "You can only use your magic on yourself or inanimate objects."

"I'm not sorry." I shook my head and looked around the room. "I'll do it again."

Max stepped between Elsie and me, facing her. Whatever the look was that he gave her had her hard stance soften just a smidge before dropping her arms to her sides.

"We have rules we must live by," she said a bit calmer.

"I get that. And I also get the morality of what you're saying. But these people were only dead because of their proximity to me. I couldn't be the reason they died."

"It's imperative you promise me right now you won't do any magic unless you run it by me first."

"No way." I laughed. "This is mine. It's part of me. Not you, nor anyone else, will tell me how or when to use it." I stepped forward, and in a voice, I'd only learned existed inside of me that day said, "You'll not mute my magic like before."

"You brought people back from the dead, Witch!" she yelled in a more impressive other worldly voice than mine. She also had glowing eyes that conveyed all the anger and disappointment she was feeling toward me.

I was the first of the Thirteen witches, and they needed me to be strong. I saw firsthand what they were up against, and I knew how much was weighing on my shoulders. How could I not? The pressure was immense.

Elsie took a deep breath and pinched the bridge of her nose. "I understand and am very happy you've come into your magic so beautifully. But you must understand that every single thing you do has a consequence. Sometimes, other people, innocent people, reap the blowback of your actions. And that's when the darkness sets in... and the change begins.

We all walk a fine line between light and dark. Good and evil."

She spread her arms wide. "If you practice dark magic, you will become dark. No two ways about it. You'll begin to believe you know what's best, your way is easiest. Everyone will simply be happier if you handle their things for them. But it never ever stops there. Ever. And before you know it, you will no longer even care if they benefit from your magic. It's much easier to do whatever you want; when you want. For everyone's own good, of course. After all, what value is there really with individual freedom and personal choice, when you," she gestured to me, "the great and wise witch Cassandra, already know what's best for everyone?"

She stepped closer to me and put her finger in my face. "And that, little witch, is how sorcery is born. I'll not be associated with a sorcerer."

My stomach dropped, and I wove my fingers through Thaddeus'.

Her words had value and made sense, but I stood firm.

"I don't regret saving him," I whispered, and squeezed his hand.

"You shouldn't have done it."

"How could I not?" I cried. "He fought hard and gave his life to save mine when the monster was trying to drag me back into the lake with it. How could I do anything short of bringing him back?"

I would never tell anyone I'd truthfully brought them all back.

"How is that wrong in any stretch of the imagination? And not just that, why aren't we curing world hunger... and cancer? What is wrong with us, that we aren't stopping the suffering now when we have the ability at our fingertips. Literally?"

She pointed to the bookshelves across the room. "You will read volumes seven, nine, and twelve, of *Lestiminti le vimfi* and then tell me why we cannot interfere in humankind." She watched me for a beat then looked at Thaddeus, and back to me.

"You are a witch. Witches do no harm." She moved to Thaddeus and like she hadn't just balled me out, said, "I'd like to run some tests on you."

"Wait," Max said. "Thaddeus also pledged his loyalty and guardianship to Cassandra."

"Is this true?" Elsie asked me.

I nodded unsure if I was in for more trouble, and I was certainly not going to tell them that I'd said for him to do that when I brought him back. I needed to know if he truly wanted to be paired with me or if it was my own words that demanded the pledge from him. I had to know it was of his own free will. Otherwise, I didn't want it.

"If he truly wants to be my guardian, then I would be honored." I hoped that set the intention back in his court, and he wasn't unduly influenced by my words at the lake. It also brought clearer how important free will was and how careful I needed to be with my power.

"Good. Do you accept his devotion to you?"

That sounded pretty deep. I wasn't sure if I was up for anything long-term, even if it was of his own free will.

I looked at Thaddeus. He was super-hot, and I had saved his life because he had died trying to save mine. I think that made me responsible for him now or something.

Relationships had been built on less. I'd kept myself separated from the world long enough. Now was my chance to belong. And belong to something important.

I nodded yes and felt Thaddeus relax. I definitely needed to learn the rules around here. Especially if someone else was going to be tied to me. Poor guy. I was probably going to get us both into a lot of trouble before it was all said and done.

"Good. But before we move forward teaching her about the bonding ritual, she must get caught up on witch history, and why we don't meddle. I won't do another thing with her until that is done." Elsie turned her back to me and faced my potential guardian. "Thaddeus, until the ceremony, you're still a free wolf. Come with me."

Elsie walked to the bookshelf and pulled three large tomes from their place. The bindings were worn from years of use. If this was some sort of punishment, she was way off base. Little did she know I couldn't wait to get my hands on them. Luckily for me, reading was one of my favorite pastimes. It's what happens when you don't have any friends or family. Seems not much would change here about that either. Except for Thaddeus. I'd have him.

***

I tested my blood and was thrilled to find that even though my eating was sporadic, my levels were in the normal range and that had never happened to me before. It did occur to me I could wish my diabetes away, but since I was forbidden to do any magic, I held myself in check. I spent the next several days trying to read the volumes of witch history. Much of it I didn't understand because, even though they were written in some form of English, it was a version of English that required a bunch of searching the internet for words I'd never seen before. There were extra characters in this alphabet and punctuation that was foreign to me. Some of the time I could grab the gist because of the context they might have been used in, but even that was spotty. There was a lot of guesswork. It was a slow and frustrating endeavor. I'd resigned myself that I was going to have to confess to Elsie that I wasn't able to get as much from them as she'd hoped. From what I'd gathered, witches, for the most part, were the only reason humanity even survived. Humans were constantly on the brink of extinction due to plague, war, filthy living conditions, and famine. The witches were sympathetic to the plight of the lesser species and taught the women of the tribes and villages how to heal the sick, use herbs and energy stones to cleanse wounds, safely deliver babies, and the importance of proper diet. They taught them how to preserve food to last throughout the winter, salt meats, and pickle crops. The witches were the inventors of mead which later became ale and then much later beer. The early witches passed the brewing techniques down to the human females only.

I thought it odd that there was no mention of teaching or training men. Seems they mistrusted human men, or maybe it was simply a sign of the times at hand. Men and women did not share space or chores back then. Either way, it proved to be good instincts, but also their downfall. Human males soon became jealous and envious of the knowledge that was only passed onto human females. It was also a means to some sort of feminine independence that didn't exist in that time. If women were valued, they had a place in the village or tribe. If they had the protection of the whole village that meant they weren't dependent upon a male for their survival.

Witches had contributed so much to humanity, only to have their hard work turned against them. I read of torture and cruelty of which I'd never heard before. This history certainly wasn't in any of the textbooks or taught in any of the classes I'd attended.

And through it all, witches never fought back. One recurring phrase appeared over and over throughout all three tomes: "Do No Harm". From the stories recounted in the thick uneven pages, I learned of the women who had come before me. I read about those who had sacrificed so much so the humans might prosper and thrive. I cried, laughed, and experienced serious light bulb moments learning how things I took for granted today were life-saving measures back then. Chills ran over my skin as I read on to events and actions that would change me permanently...forever.

I delved into a section entitled 'Blood Wars.' Once there, I lost track of time as I was deeply sucked into the gruesome story that unfolded before me. The persecution of the witches by the Church in Europe. How fear spread quickly across the continent, encompassing horrible cruelty born from revenge and greed.

How the vampire race whispered falsehoods and fear into the minds of man and turned the entire human race against the witches and any human who practiced their healing craft. Eventually, they drove the witches from their homes and across the sea to the New World, where they lived in harmony for many centuries with the nomadic indigenous people of the Great Plains and beyond. That is until the European settlers arrived. The witch population withdrew and isolated themselves but that wasn't enough. Soon, the persecution and devastation of the witch trials and later witch-burning would rear its ugly head until finally there were only fourteen witches left in all of the world.

And they were being hunted to extinction.

As a last-ditch effort to save Witchkind, their souls were 'stored' away in a death slumber. Only to arise when needed the most. Which brought us to today. The Thornwood Thirteen was to be their salvation. And I had a lot of redeeming to do. I felt sick to my stomach when I thought about the fact that vampires were our arch-enemy, only interested in furthering their own agenda. They were the root cause of the persecution of witches. Chauvinistic BS, I'd say. I shivered when I thought how close I'd let Rolfe near me. He wanted to sell me to his court, whatever that meant. After reading the tomes, I realized what he'd meant for me. I'd have suffered horrific acts of torture, and he knew it.

I needed to know more. Now that I knew our history, I wanted to know about the other magical beings and how they helped or harmed us. I felt a desperation wash over me not to let my sisters down. I had to learn where my place was so I could make sure I was part of the solution and not just another problem heaped on top of the mountain of problems we already faced.

First, I was still fuzzy on why I shouldn't have brought Thaddeus and Mr. Miller back to life. Yes, I now understood the concept of death magic and learned much from the tomes about it. But what my magic did was not death magic. My subjects didn't reanimate, they were restored to *before.* I wanted to give Elsie the benefit of the doubt. I was one hundred percent certain she was coming from an authentic place. I just needed to discuss it further, if she was open. Convince her to see the value in the gift I'd been given.

After wandering the manor for almost an hour and getting delightfully lost a couple of times; the manor was a whole-body experience - not just a house but it actually felt alive and active; I knew deep in the recesses of my being I was home. Home.

Something I'd never really felt before regardless of how cute I made the condo where I lived.

I eventually found her in what was, for all intents and purposes, a large glass greenhouse that jutted out off of the back of Thornwood.

Like everything at Thornwood manor, it was also extra awesome and straight out of a Gothic movie. The shape of the glass building was that of a chapel complete with a tall spiky iron weather vane at its peak. I entered the building quietly and was assaulted by an overwhelming mixture of fragrances. The four walls were lined with plants and shelves of glass bottles in multiple shapes, sizes, and colors. Herbs, flowers, and twigs were hanging from decorative rods that ran the length of the room. Half looked dried and the other half looked like they were still working on the process of becoming so.

"Elsie," I asked.

The rows of potted shelves made it hard to see anyone in the room unless you shared a row with them.

"Here," I heard her mumble and then saw Max's head peek from the end of the next row over.

I came to realize after the first couple of days that Max was never far from Elsie. It didn't seem likely they shared a sleeping space, but it was unmistakable that they were a couple. I also came to realize the way I thought of couples in human capacity was much different than how old-as-dirt magical people acted in couple form.

Also, the wolves slept outdoors. Like, in the forest. There were about thirty of the large hunks and a handful of younglings (that's what Elsie called them), but as the sun readied to set, they slowly disappeared. All but Max and Thaddeus.

Honestly, I had no idea where Max slept; it wasn't really my business, but this girl could be nosey. Thaddeus, I knew, slept in one of the converted outbuildings. The wolves had claimed several of them and set up lockers and living quarters for when the weather turned sour.

I rounded the end of the row to find Elsie at a long gardening bench, dressed in a long-sleeved blue dress with red rubber boots, green gloves, and clear goggles. Her multitude of braids were uncharacteristically loose and hung long down her back. I'd never seen her hair down, and my hands itched to reach out and touch it.

She was preoccupied with the process of grinding a mortar into a pestle that held various dried plants she'd strung out across her workspace. She had one of her large leather-bound hand-sewn books alongside that she was pasting bits of the plants into and making notes.

Max leaned down to me and said, "There is no better way of learning than to step in and lend a hand."

It was good advice, so that's what I did.

Chapter 21

Emotions are contagious! Avoid angry people at all cost. Seek happiness for

your own wellbeing.

Elsie spent the next several days doing the best job she could
of putting me through a rigorous crash course of enhancing
my marking abilities. We needed me to a point where I could
mark my guardian (when one eventually stepped forward... if
one stepped forward) so he could shift into other creatures. It
wasn't just for my safety, but also for the safety of those who
resided at the manor. The bonded wolves would be the ones
who remained behind to protect Thornwood while the
unbonded sought the awakening sister witches. I'd also be
able to add runes of protection to the wolf targeting a number
of different foes.

It was crucial I learn as quickly as possible. Luckily, I was
allowed to study Max's, as he was the only wolf marked with
anything more than protection.

I learned from her how important placement, chanting tone, and abundance of *maginka* was. Luckily, for any that would be my guardian, I knew how to draw and would be able to give good tattoos. They'd be stuck with them their whole lives, so I didn't want to give them anything they would be embarrassed by. Seems I was the only one worried about the appearance. Apparently, once the marking was applied, it took its own shape, so even the crudest of markings would look like the spell, not what I tattooed. For example, all bird marks that allowed the shifter to transform into a large bird of prey looked very similar to every other one, regardless of who did the marking. It was a witchy thing I didn't fully understand but wasn't crucial to our survival so the why was deemed unnecessary, for now.

I learned everything I could and tried to get to know the wolves by name. They were all very handsome and extremely friendly. Extremely eager to help and lend a hand in anything I worked on.

I met the wood fairies that lived on the estate and managed Elsie's deadly garden, which I was forbidden to visit. I hated the fact, it only made me want to go see it more once I'd learned it was strictly prohibited.

We'd figured the black soldier who had appeared before we made it to Thornwood was a tracker. Necromancy, I learned, was dirty magic and to be feared. It corrupted any and all who came in contact with it.

Thaddeus and I had grown closer as well over the last few days. He hadn't brought up the bonding again since the talk with Elsie, and while I was disappointed he didn't want to be my guardian, I wouldn't hold it against him. I figured he was holding out to see the other witches as they awoke. Why be stuck with me when he could have a witch who was so much better?

I knew I had a long road ahead of me and that I hadn't gotten off on the right foot with Elsie, but she didn't seem to be holding it against me.

I still felt my magic was good and pure, and I couldn't swear to her I wouldn't bring her back if she died. I didn't tell her that because why argue about something that hadn't happened yet?

My old witch soul told me this was an argument that had been waged many times before and would be many times in the future.

Speaking of my old witch soul, she and I were getting to know each other rather well. Her memories were coming to me in bits and pieces, but I'd say the strongest influence she had was her feelings. When I felt an emotion associated with my magic, that was when I felt the strongest connection to her.

She had been shut out and shut down so many times she was sad now. She'd never been able to live out her best life. First, she was born of a time when men oppressed women, but when her own coven oppressed her magic from fear and hysteria, it left her living a life unfulfilled. And she, we, had so much to offer. I promised her I would be strong for us both. My hair had become a topic, Elsie said a witch's hair was the basis of her magic, and I was never to cut it again. I guess that explained her miles and miles of braids. Mine was also my magical tell like her eyes were. The tips of my hair glowed non-stop now and would brighten up when I was using my magic or became emotional. She said I needed to pay attention to the glowing because it would help me in the future. She also said it would help any guardian who wished to bond with me. They'd be able to read me by my magical tell.

Apparently, witch magic took a toll on the user, that was why I'd been suffering from headaches and tingling fingertips. The more powerful I become the less harm I would cause to myself when I used my power. I'd need to use talismans, spells, and charms to minimize the backlash. Speaking of talismans; my pendant suffered intense inspections, which turned into experiments, and finally, a determination was made by the Last Witch that it was pure witch magic and once I cleansed it, should become part of my magical toolbox. It was my first ritualistic cleansing, under a full moon in the ocean, and I loved it.

Basically, my days consisted of learning and doing spell work. I was given my first blank hand-sewn book and was told to get started on my own Book of Shadows. She walked me through the vast library that spanned several rooms which held all the grimoires from witches past, full of spells, incantations, and rituals. I learned a completed spell book became a grimoire and was used for reference, and the current book a witch worked on was her Book of Shadows.

I was assigned a garden and instructed to learn everything that was planted in it and why. I loved sinking my hands into the rich soil, and delighted with satisfaction when my herbs bloomed under my care. She had me working on crystals in the moonlight, which I washed and cleansed in the saltwater of the ocean, just like the pendant. Crystal work came after dinner, gardening in the morning, and afternoons were for spell work.

I fell into a nice rhythm.

The estate was a busy place, and all seemed to flow well together. The only real downside was no one had stepped up to become my guardian. I supposed the news had gotten out.

I had practiced magic I wasn't supposed to and the wolves didn't want me.

It hurt, but who could blame them. And after all, why should my witchy life be any different than my human life? Yeah, I knew I was in the middle of a full-blown pity party, but I couldn't seem to quiet the voices in my head that had been telling me my whole life I wasn't enough.

I would never be enough.

I'd spend early mornings on a peak overlooking the Pacific Ocean. I'd climb to the tip of the cliff, and out onto a rock that jutted over the ocean just before the sun crested the sky. I'd wait for its new rays to hit my face and I'd exhale. This was where I truly belonged. The waves crashing against the rocks were mesmerizing. The sea spray occasionally misting my face was oddly comforting. If I were meant to live my life alone this was going to be an acceptable place to do it.

No one knew I climbed to the peak to welcome in the day. It was my little slice of heaven.

Mine alone.

Chapter 22

Wear a piece of moonstone jewelry to help with fertility, passion,

and love.

He owed her his life. He'd been watching the new witch

since they arrived back at the manor. Everything she did was

perfect. Cassandra didn't have a nefarious bone in her

beautiful body. He'd swear on it with his last breath.

He couldn't explain what had happened but he knew it was

not death magic. He also knew she'd do it again. And that

might get her killed or even worse, banished. Meaning her

soul would never be reborn. He couldn't let that happen. Not

after everything she'd done for him.

He'd dedicate himself to her, and once he made that pledge,

the deal would be done.

Thaddeus kept his eyes on the witch that had come to mean

everything to him. He watched as she stole away to her cliff to

watch the sunrise. He watched as she poured over her Book of

Shadows. It took every bit of restraint on his part not to rush to take the tools from her blistered hands as she gardened long hours. He sat in the shadows during the moonlight rituals as she worked her incantations over her powerful crystals.

It didn't matter to him what happened with her, he would be there. Quietly waiting for her to be ready to receive him.

He didn't need the bonding ceremony to solidify his devotion to her. It was going to be up to him to help her transition to her new world and the new power she wielded. He wanted nothing more than to see her succeed.

With that in mind, Thaddeus went in search of the beautiful woman with the strikingly unusual hair that glowed when she spoke her influence. She'd been assigned to learn her history before the Last Witch would take her any further. And she did, brilliantly. She was smart and studied hard. His chest swelled with pride. He already thought of her as his.

Thaddeus was pleased that Cassandra was learning so much so quickly, but he did find fault in the Last Witch's dismissal of Cassandra's most impressive gift.

Facts were facts. It was not necromancy that brought him back. It was something clean and good. Not dark and evil. He thought it a grave mistake to discount her ability. After all, with them so crazily outnumbered, they needed an ace in the hole, and he knew in his soul, she was it. He exhausted himself pleading her case to both Maximillian and Elsie. The Vampire alone outnumbered them a hundred to one. And the bloodsuckers weren't even in the war yet, from what they could tell. It was smart of his witch to make the vamp forget her. She had good instincts.

He found Max exiting the glasshouse.

"I'd like to speak with you and Elsie about Cassandra and the bonding ceremony."

Max placed his hand on Thaddeus' shoulder. "They're working on new ingredient combinations for *marking* spells now. Can it wait?" Max dropped his hand and turned towards the tomato garden.

Thaddeus fell into step next to Max. "I'd rather not wait. I mean, I don't want to rush her, I'm doing everything in my power to be patient, but I feel the weight of impending doom crushing my spirit."

"Yes, I feel it too."

Max opened the gate to the nightshade garden and sought the variety he'd been sent to retrieve. Thaddeus watched Max walk the length of the impressive plot and pitched off to the left, only to return to the main path empty-handed. Thaddeus observed him do this several more times before he heard Max yell, "Eureka!" And returned to view with an armful of large purple tomatoes.

"How can you go about like a war isn't being waged at our very doorstep?"

Max studied Thaddeus for a moment, shook his head, and without replying headed back to the glasshouse with Thaddeus hot on his heels.

"She needs to have the strength of a guardian before the next battle," Thaddeus said.

"Indeed, she does." Max didn't slow his stride.

"Well?" Thaddeus was trying to be patient but something had to give. He didn't want to push, but he *needed* her protected.

Max stopped at the door of the glasshouse. "Wolf, you have been dragging your heels like a youngling who couldn't make up his own mind for weeks. And now you want to lay it at my feet," He scoffed. "Bond with the witch already. She's been waiting, Elsie has been waiting, I've been waiting... We've all been waiting for you to make a move. Do you have any idea how many wolves I've made to wait for you to pull your head out of the dirt? Forsakes! Put us out of our misery!"

Thaddeus was in stunned silence as Max wretched the door open and announced success in his tomato quest. He held two of the dark purple nightshade fruits up high and received a bright smile from Elsie.

The witches were both wearing protective eyewear and gloves. They'd had their heads together, and Cassandra held a large book in her arms that she appeared to be writing notes in. Elsie looked back and continued the conversation the two witches had been having before the wolves appeared.

"Potions aren't about exact measurements. Spell measurements are more in line with a pinch, a scoop, a twig or leaf, and even a sprinkle. We don't use measuring tools or spoons, or any such objects. Every witch has her own version of every spell."

Elsie picked up a thick glass vial filled with black liquid. "Take this, for example. *Maginka* it's what I use to mark Max and the other wolves with protection runes. And it will work very nicely for your bonding ceremony to Thaddeus. But it's mine and made for my magic. When you brew your own, it will have the same ingredients, but maybe your pinches are a tiny bit larger than mine, or your breath is warmer and deeper when you chant your incantations. This is where your magic recognizes the pathways you've created for it. You can use other witches' spells and potions, but yours will be oh so much better for you than anyone else's will ever be. Do you understand?"

"Yes, magic is individualistic."

"Yes, exactly. You've got it, don't you?"

"I think so. Should I be brewing up my own batch of ink to use?" Cassandra asked, reaching for the vial.

Elsie kept her eyes on the thick seeded glass as it passed from her hand to the young witch.

"While that would be ideal, we simply don't have enough time. We need you bonded to at least one guardian before the next awakening, and you'll need to start bestowing your gifts upon him as quickly as you can. Besides, it has to brew over a redwood open flame fire for seven nights in which the final night must be a new moon. So that's a bit of a hiccup."

"But can we get it ready for the next new moon?"

"Absolutely. Right now, let's start your preparation for the bonding ritual. I believe your wolf is anxious to be on the other side of his status in limbo." She turned and smirked at Thaddeus who hovered in the doorway.

"So, I'll use this?" Cassandra held the *maginka* up and let the light filter through it.

Her arm was brought down sharply by the Last Witch. "Keep it away from the sunlight, girl. You're going to undo months of hard work for that small vial."

"Oh," she said and held it up again, this time careful not to let the sun hit it. "It's beautiful."

The black ink had a pearlescence quality that glimmered as it moved back and forth inside the vial with a syrupy consistency.

"That vial has been curing for seven years. Not very long, as potions go, but long enough to be extremely effective," Elsie said.

"Seven years? That means I better get some potions made so they can start curing or I'll never have my own to work with." Cassandra grabbed a glass bottle and poured the mixture she'd been working on into the vial and capped it. Then she found a cupboard to store it in.

"I'll use this cabinet. What's next?"

Elsie looked toward the wolves.

"I've been researching the death slumber participants and along with your ability of influence and your unusual hair, my assumption is that your original witch soul belonged to Serafina the Silent." Elsie's smile showed a lot of teeth, and while it was intended to portray happiness, it came off looking predatory.

"Close your eyes," Elsie said.

Once Cassandra's eyes were shut the Last Witch uncorked a vial of ash and smudged a line with two squiggly lines across it on her forehead. "*Livita lorelie* Serafina."

Magic powered the rune, and Cassandra took a step back as images flooded her mind of olden times, she knew she'd never seen before. She felt desperation and loneliness wash over her the likes she'd never known in her whole life. Tears streamed down her face, and she knew she was in fact Serafina the Silent, and she'd hated that name.

The only reason she'd been quiet was that she'd been shamed by the coven to remain so. They were afraid of her power. They feared her voice and its influence. So, like a good little witch, she did as she was told and isolated herself away. She wasn't one of the first solitary witches, but she certainly understood the appeal.

Cassandra turned on her heel as the images and emotions flooded her system. She ran as fast as she could away from the glasshouse and the witch that knew her before. It was more than just the memories, she felt Serafina. Felt her loneliness and despair. Felt how disconnected to the coven she'd been made to feel.

Cassandra didn't pay attention to where she was going as she ran away. But she knew exactly where she was when she flopped down on the hard stone peak overlooking an angry ocean. The sun was just preparing to set after a long day and somehow felt fitting that she see the sun leave the sky from the exact place she'll be greeting it again the next morning. There was magic and rhythm to it.

Sadly, most of her coven had been burned at the stake or hanged from an old wooden bridge near their village. When she'd been presented the opportunity to reawaken at a later time, she grabbed hold of it and never doubted herself. She saw her rune in her mind's eye and knew that was her power point.

She looked to Thaddeus.

Cassandra wasn't surprised when he landed next to her. He wrapped his arm around her waist and held her as she wept for the past, and cried for the future.

"I know who I am," Cassandra whispered to Thaddeus, her eyes fixed upon him. "I am strong and valuable but she will try to silence me when I am needed most."

"Then we must show her your strength." Thaddeus never wavered. "Your magic is pure light. There is nothing dark or sinister about it. Just because she doesn't understand it doesn't make it wrong or evil."

Cassandra stopped crying and saw him for who he truly was. Her voice quivered when she asked the question she'd wanted to ask since they arrived at Thornwood, "will you bond with me?"

"I thought you'd never ask," his breath rushed out.

"I was waiting for you."

"I was waiting for you. The witch has the final say," He took her hand. "I thought I'd been clear. I will always remain by your side. Bonded or not."

"I want you there too." A flash distracted the couple as the sun set deep past the ocean and pitched them into night.

"We'd better get back. My exit wasn't very impressive," Cassandra drawled.

"I dunno, I kind of enjoyed the jog," Thaddeus laughed and walked his witch back to the greenhouse.

Cassandra and Thaddeus found Max and Elsie exactly where they'd left them in a small argument.

"That's not what I said!" Elsie exclaimed through clenched teeth. The elder couple stopped speaking immediately as the greenhouse door opened and smiled the worst fake smiles ever known to witch and wolfkind.

"I will not be silenced again," Cassandra announced. Better to get it out in the open. There would be no more hiding who she was.

Max went still and Thaddeus braced behind her. Thaddeus didn't want to go against his Alpha but for this tiny witch, he would.

The Last Witch bowed her head to Cassandra. "After inspecting Thaddeus, I must agree that your form of magic is definitely not necromancy... and as much as it pains me to say, we may need to consider it... you... your magic... as a tool instead of something to fear. That was a problem with the ancient witches. They had rules, commandments truly... and they were unbending in their pursuit of adhering to them. Looking back, I think they were fools and were the reason we almost vanished completely.

"I," Elsie placed her hand on her own chest, "while an elder witch now, was a young witch when the death slumber was enacted. Although powerful for my age, it was my ability to learn and adapt quickly that was the sole reason I was chosen to live out the long years awaiting the time for the awakening and bring it forth. They thought I had the best chances of surviving the centuries we all believed we needed."

"You've been by yourself? All alone, for centuries?"

"Yes, and while I'd love nothing more than to regale you with stories of the decades that dragged along one sunrise at a time... and of my lingering in sheer boredom with no end in sight... I, my dear, have been very busy preparing for the war to come."

She whipped her gloves off. "Now that we know who you are, let's get you bonded with Thaddeus, your handsome guardian, and then teach you how to *mark* him so that he can protect you effectively."

She turned to Thaddeus, "Are you ready for me?" Cassandra asked quietly. He placed his arm across her shoulders and pulled her into his embrace.

His hug and the Last Witch's laughter was the only answer she needed.

"Come on, let's get you dressed. You're about to experience one of the best things about being a witch." Elsie tugged the newly awakened witch from Thaddeus and looped her arm through Cassandra's.

"Is that right?" Max growled. "One of the best things, you say? Is that why you were able to remain separated from me for so long?" He turned on his heel and slammed out of the glass building.

The witches had forgotten the wolves were listening.

"We were already arguing." Elsie's eyes swiveled to Cassandra. "You should know; wolves are emotional."

Chapter 23

Place an amethyst next to your bed to help with dreamwork.

The bonding ceremony was performed in private in the

forest. Nature was to be their witness and nature alone. It was

no one's business what transpired between a witch and her

wolf.

Cassandra was in a long flowing dress with an elaborate train

that featured her rune in silver thread. The stunning dress

was sage green and made of a soft earthy gauze. It was

lightweight and slightly see-through. She'd objected to the

garment at first, but once she saw how beautiful it looked on

her, she decided not to be so modest and dressed in it

happily.

The ceremony was short; the pair walked along the blessed

path hand in hand until it opened up to a sacred spot in the

forest denoted by tall blue flowers and blue crystals that

surrounded an open structure. Several birch trees had been woven together during growth and now a living growing gazebo stood in the powerful space. The same blue flowers that surrounded the birch wood were woven throughout the branches. Blue crystals hung at varying heights from the ceiling and glowed softly.

Thaddeus was dressed in a pair of black slacks and a black button-up shirt with silver metal buttons and cufflinks. Cassandra carried a ceremonial dagger made of bone that Thaddeus had carved her rune into and then poured molten silver in the carving to enhance its power.

The world faded away as the two spoke words of promise and dedication. Elsie had said the words themselves mattered little, as long as the intention was there.

Thaddeus promised to protect his witch with his life, and Cassandra promised to bring him back every single time he did.

They both laughed.

 Next, she used the tip of the dagger she'd dipped into a potion she'd brewed herself that morning. Holding his hand she traced a line with a swish and a smaller squiggly line across it, into his left palm and forehead. Once her rune had been traced, she spoke the incantation Elsie had given her.

"Infiniti semi levastipo bemina ferva."

The crystals glowed brightly, and many more flowers on the branches bloomed, larger than the ones before.

Blue light surrounded the couple, and for a brief moment, neither could move as their heartbeats synced with one another. As soon as their two hearts beat as one, their emotions merged. A powerful blue light swirled around their bodies as Thaddeus pulled Cassandra to him. She felt his incredible inner strength, and also his fear for her survival. He'd do anything to keep her alive. He would care for her better than she would care for herself.

Thaddeus felt Cassandra's devotion and her strong sense of justice. He knew even if it cost her, she would do everything in her power to save him and keep him close to her. She would always follow the path of righteousness.

Thaddeus held her tighter and looked down into her upturned face.

"I've finally found my home," he whispered. "The place I belong. Thank you for giving me a purpose and a place. I wander no more seeking what is mine. I've been waiting for you for so long." He buried his face in her neck. "I finally found you. I am home."

Cassandra was overcome with the emotions she could feel from Thaddeus. She clung to him and wept. Words were pointless; he could feel her, even if the words wouldn't form. He used his thumb to wipe a tear from under her eye.

"I love you," she whispered.

Thaddeus threw his head back and laughed. "So, you do, little one."

He kissed the top of her head, and the blue glow slowly receded. The crystals dimmed to their original levels and the blue flowers that had bloomed around them on the birchwood structure folded back into buds.

The ceremony completed, the pair headed back, arm in arm, to Thornwood Manor to celebrate with the wolves and prepare for their first marking as a bonded couple.

The giant bonfire came into view. They could smell the roasting meat, and Cassandra's mouth watered.

"What smells so good?"

"I believe it's several rabbits and a deer," Thaddeus remarked.

Cassandra didn't think that sounded good. "Will there be other things to eat?"

"The witches I've known have been what you'd refer to as vegan in modern times."

"I'm not vegan. I like seafood. But I'm not into eating rabbits or deer."

Thaddeus laughed again. "I'll take you to the wharf tomorrow, and we'll load up on fresh seafood we can freeze, so you don't run out."

She squeezed his arm and changed the subject.

"What do you want to shift into first?" Cassandra asked.

"A giant bird," Thaddeus replied.

"A bird?"

"Yes, I want to soar above the treetops."

"So, it shall be."

****

Elsie, the Last Witch, sipped hot tea from her favorite mug as she held her scrying stone over the newest map she'd made. She'd been doing this act three times a day for weeks with no new activity.

She performed the spell to gently awaken one more soul. This time, she tried targeting a soul specifically. Lisbette the Gifted. She was one of the best spell workers Elsie had ever known and would be invaluable in helping to teach and corral the other witches as they were awoken and brought to the manor.

Lisbette's magic had been of empathy and justice. She could feel and influence another's emotions and tell when someone was lying. She was a master spell worker and made charms and talismans that held magic unmatched to this day.

She lowered the rough-cut diamond over the map and took another sip.

The diamond began spinning on its own, and the Last Witch slammed her cup down on the edge of the round table, splashing hot tea, just as the stone was ripped from her fingers to land hard on a small area deep in the state of Louisiana.

Elsie peered closer. She was just outside of Baton Rouge. Old forms of Death Magic were worshiped, practiced, and even commercialized in this region of the New World. Spirits and souls from the past who never moved on tended to concentrate in the older cemeteries and the Deep South was full of them. Plenty of candidates for their enemy to form an undead army against her.

"Max!" she shouted. "Gather the wolves!"

***

Cassandra watched as the giant bird soared above the waves as they crashed against the shoreline. Pride swelled in her chest as she wondered at the beauty of the bird in flight. She'd done that. She'd given her beloved Thaddeus the wings to fly. She couldn't wait to give him more. Any creature he wanted to be she would gift to him.

Their connection had been one of the highlights of her life. After living in solitude, she finally belonged to one person who would take her any way she came.

She didn't have to work to be perfect for him, he already thought her so. She knew because the bond gave them both the ability to feel each other.

The way he felt about her was overwhelming. Sometimes, it took her breath away.

"Cassandra!" Elsie screamed in her head, "Another has awoken! Come quick! And bring your wolf down from the sky, we need you both!"

Chapter 24

In all things; Do No Harm.

"**Y**ou failed me, you worthless dung heap." Master Ziefrus

brought his arm back to strike the utter disappointment that

once called himself Sigt.

The flayed creature howled in pain as the razor-sharp whip

struck his skinless back once more.

"The first of the Thirteen has managed to subvert your best

efforts and is now laughing it up with the Last Witch at

Thornwood Manor!" Master Ziefrus yelled, spittle flying as he

brought the blood drawing weapon down on his victim's back

for the one hundred and seventy-fourth time.

"Gi...give me another chance, Master!" Sigt wailed.

"Do you think I'd give you another chance to screw things up?

No, I have another in mind. This is too important to leave to

the likes of you... you disgust me," Master Ziefrus snarled.

"Slagnt!" Master Ziefrus bellowed, and a giant oozing troll promptly appeared.

"Master," Slagnt bowed low to his master.

"Take over the punishment. I can't be bothered with him," Master Ziefrus spat on his disappointing former lieutenant. "Don't stop until he dies. When he does, call me. Maybe reanimating him will make him more useful."

"Please, Master, no," the pitiful creature begged for his life as Master Ziefrus stomped away, his boots splashing through the sludge of decay and past the cage-lined hall.

"The Oracle wishes your presence, Master," a cowering serpent hissed.

Master Ziefrus spun on his heel and headed toward the crude stairwell that led down to the Oracle's cell.

The cages fell silent once more as he passed. He was the only being that no arms reached for as he walked by the rows and rows of metal boxes. The occupants knew good and well their time with the Master would come eventually, and when it did, that time would not only be their last but also, the worst.

Their end would be horrific at the hands of the Master Necromancer.

He stormed down the uneven stairs in a silent rage. How dare his best soldier fail him so terribly!

"You'd better have good news for me, or I'll be peeling your hide from your grotesque body myself!" he bellowed.

The Oracle slithered out from the shadows where it stayed most of the time the Necromancer was in its presence.

"Another is awakening."

"The second of the Thirteen?"

"Yes. Her location is on the map."

"Are you positive?"

"The magic is witch."

"You better be right."

"Master, I'm always right," the Oracle said and slithered back into the shadow.

Master Ziefrus had half a mind to rid the entire cavern of darkness so it couldn't shield itself from him again and then decided he'd use it as punishment in the future.

The thought of hurting the Oracle brought a measure of calm to him.

Now, to get that witch!

"Bitsogn! Summon the Death Ravens!"

Cool Stuff

Come join me on social media,

Facebook: T Wells Brown

Instagram: @Twellsbrown

Twitter: @twellsbrown

Book Bub: Author T Wells Brown

Stay in the know by signing up for my Newsletter:

www.womenofwinecountry.com

Please follow my author page on
Amazon @ T Wells Brown

Stay tuned for the next volume of the Earth Magic
saga: Sharp Stones coming Spring 2022

A note from the author

Thank you for reading my first modern fantasy book. I hope you enjoyed reading it as much as I enjoyed writing it. Fantasy has been my preferred genre to read in all of its glorious subcategories. From Paranormal Romance, to High Fantasy, to our modern time Urban Fantasy, I love them all.

My absolute favorite trope is the unsuspecting mortal who discovers powers they never knew they had, and uses said powers to defeat the treacherous villain. LOVE.

I hope you'll check out some of my other books, but if those don't tickle your fancy, I hope you'll stay tuned for the next installment of the Earth Magic saga.

xoxo T Wells Brown